Cold Town

Also by Sarah Diamond

The Beach Road

Cold Town

Sarah Diamond

First published in Great Britain in 2001 by Orion,
an imprint of the Orion Publishing Group Ltd.

A CIP catalogue record for this book
is available from the British Library.

ISBN (hardback) 075283 785 0
ISBN (paperback) 075284 625 6

Typeset by Deltatype, Birkenhead, Wirral

Set in $11\frac{1}{2}/14\frac{1}{2}$ Minion

Printed in Great Britain by
Clays Ltd, St Ives plc

The Orion Publishing Group Ltd
Orion House
5 Upper Saint Martin's Lane
London, WC2H 9EA

For Catherine

Prologue

The boy stood in the orchard that led on from the vicarage garden. Overhead, the sun blazed down from a cloudless blue sky, and fat cartoonish bees thrummed and hovered round the wildflowers. Far away on the quiet afternoon came the murmured hint of a cricket match. The boy heard none of it. He stood and looked down, and the sound of his own breathing was the only sound in the world.

His sister lay against the trunk of an apple tree, unmoving. She might have been resting after a strenuous game of hide-and-seek, and the image one of inviolate childish innocence – the bright sunlight gleamed off her long butter-coloured plaits, her red-and-white gingham dress. But her wide blue eyes stared blindly into space, and the marks on her neck were livid.

Her skipping-rope lay in the long grass beside her, coiled like a snake. The boy stood and looked down at her with a strange expression in his eyes. Perhaps it was joy, perhaps terror – or, perhaps, an awful combination of the two.

He stood where he was for another few seconds, then turned and ran, his footsteps rustling the grass. The sun blazed down on buttercups and daisies and shiny red apples, and a little murdered girl named Katie Fielding, whom her parents had loved more than anyone in the world.

Then the boy's footsteps faded, and the silence began.

Book One

1

When Terry came out of the seven-storey building in Soho Square, it was almost six o'clock. He put up his umbrella and walked, surrounded by people, as well concealed as a man could be.

What's the matter, Terry? Scared of going home?

It was punishingly cold, and almost full dark. Thin, steady November drizzle slanted across grey clouds and blurred the streetlights. A thousand strangers' faces shone with rain as they moved like a tide above heavy black coat collars, into the bus shelters, towards Tottenham Court Road underground station. More and more, recently, the city he lived in had frightened him – vast, anonymous and hostile, a time and a place in which he meant nothing.

But you know there's something waiting for you, don't you? If only for five or ten minutes, you can escape from it all . . .

Terry turned down Dean Street, and into the jagged twists and turns of Soho's byways. As always, coming this way at night felt like crossing the border into a foreign land that simultaneously bewildered and welcomed him. This secret world had fascinated him ever since his company had moved offices three weeks ago – the dull red glowing sign that said MODEL and the narrow wooden stairs leading up from it, the pornographic-video store across the road, a noisy gay bar with two moustachioed, leather-clad apparitions on the door – and he quickened his pace, approaching his destination, feeling its magnetic attraction in his mind. Because the rules were different there, if any rules existed, and there was no place for the creeping, nameless malaise that plagued him.

Through the deepening night, spiky with umbrellas and

neon, Terry walked, listening to furious car horns a street or so away, pounding chart music from a crowded bar, the endless static of the rain that fell around him. Even before his private sanctuary came into view, he could see it clearly in his mind's eye – the hint of secret companionship on a stairwell leading down, the promise of warmth and rosy lights and a few minutes' forgetfulness, the twist of luminous red above the doorway that scrawled out Delilah's on the soot-coloured, ancient stone.

You're not supposed to be here, Terry, murmured the little voice at the back of his mind, but he ignored it. It had returned far too recently and unexpectedly for comfort. It scared him.

2

'What'll you have, Marie?' asked Sandra, rising from the table.

'Make mine a lager top. Oh, sod it, a glass of white wine. I should be celebrating, this evening.'

'Too right, you should,' said Cheryl. 'Head of Credit, indeed. Congratulations.'

'It's going to feel weird, having you as the boss,' said Sandra, and then she was moving through the noisy Friday-evening crowds towards the bar, and it was just Marie and Cheryl sitting together by the window.

'It is going to feel weird,' said Cheryl, and laughed. 'Tell you the truth, I'm quite jealous.'

Was she? Marie hoped not – she hated bad feelings and negative emotions. They reminded her too strongly of her vague new unease at home, her half-fears about her marriage – she remembered her husband's recent strangeness with a kind of mental shudder. 'There's no need to be,' she said, quickly. 'You know it's not going to change anything.'

'Course not,' said Cheryl, and Marie tried to forget her anxiety, and told herself there was nothing for her to worry about. She was in the Central Bar close to the office with her friends and colleagues, as she always was after work on a Friday night, and she'd just been promoted, and the atmosphere was as crowded, friendly and undemanding as it always was. There was nothing really wrong at home – everything was going fine. 'It's pissing down out there,' said Cheryl, looking out into the dark wet evening. 'Thank God I brought my brolly.'

'Yeah,' said Marie, 'me too,' and then Sandra was coming back to the table, putting down the drinks. 'Well, here's to the new Head of Credit,' said Sandra, and they laughed, raised their glasses, and drank.

'You told your Terry yet?' asked Cheryl, setting hers down.

It unsettled Marie to be reminded of him – she remembered what had happened the night before last, and immediately wished she hadn't. 'Not yet,' she said. 'Thought it'd be nicer to break the news face to face. Over dinner tonight. You know.'

'He's going to be well pleased,' said Sandra.

'Well, I don't know. His father only died last month. But perhaps it might cheer him up a bit.' Instantly, Marie regretted bringing the spectre of mortality to this cheerful celebratory place where she could escape it. Banishing it with a smile, she carried on quickly. 'Just going to the loo. Back in a minute.'

The ladies' was surprisingly quiet after the bar. Marie left the cubicle and washed her hands. The mirror showed a plumpish but still pretty woman in her early thirties, with straight dark shoulder-length hair, dimples, and hazel eyes that looked slightly anxious now that she was alone. She stopped to touch up her lipstick and mascara, then hurried back out to rejoin Cheryl and Sandra. Part of her didn't really want to leave them tonight. More than anything, she hoped that her news would make things better between herself and Terry – destroy the strangeness that had drifted between them, put an end to her creeping new half-fears of home.

3

The red-carpeted stairs were thinly but adequately lit. Terry lowered his umbrella. He negotiated the steep, narrow flight carefully, until the reception area flashed out of nowhere and took him by surprise, as it always did.

It always both shocked and enraptured him, to find this sleazy glamour tucked away inside the earth. The stairs had prepared him initially for something rather pathetic, but the expected disappointment had never come. The unnerving voice faded and died in the atmosphere and décor down here – the gleaming black desk, the shadowed, misty light, the blood-red velvet curtains that covered the walls. Occasionally, they stirred in an unfelt breeze, implying a lack of solidity behind them. A sad, elderly, lizard-like man in neat black and white sat behind the desk. He looked up at Terry and smiled. 'Good evening, sir. Can I take your coat?'

His accent was heavily Eastern European, impossible to pin down to any specific country – greasy, grating, insinuating. His foreignness warmed Terry, as everything else did here: he felt as if he'd passed into a land where the laws weren't the same, where the past didn't matter. 'Sure,' he said. 'I'll pay when I leave. Haven't got any change on me right now.'

'Very well, sir,' said the old man wearily, taking Terry's coat across the counter and turning away. 'Have a nice evening.'

Terry went through the red velvet curtains opposite the desk, and down two steps. Then he entered the place where criticisms, uncertainties and the terror of failure stopped existing, where the darkness came in like a tide and swept the world away.

Inside the club, a small, well-lit bar towered with bottles and gleaming glass and the light was rosy and flattering. Empty tables were arranged round a central dance-floor, their white cloths glowing ultraviolet. The club was quiet at this hour, as it always was when he came in, and the music was muted and relaxing. A slim, dark-haired girl in a red G-string and four-inch heels writhed alone on the dance-floor, watching herself in one mirrored wall as a disco globe rotated points of light above her. The barman broke off from polishing glasses and hurried over to serve Terry. 'What can I get you, sir?'

'Jack Daniel's on the rocks, please.'

The barman turned, poured, then handed Terry his drink. Terry paid, and watched the dark-haired girl's gyrations with a sense of longing far beyond physical lust – a hunger for something forbidden and welcoming, a million miles from home. He couldn't tell whether or not the barman recognised him. 'It gets busier,' the man said confidentially. 'Here come the girls now.'

Terry looked, anticipating the huge relief laced with disappointment. The girls were as normal as ever, he saw, as unthreatening and prosaic. There were two, emerging from a dressing room that he'd never been able to see. In their sparkly mini-dresses and chunky high-heeled sandals, they alone in this place lacked fascination – they seemed as out of place here as he did. He watched them chat indifferently as they walked towards the tables, before one seemed to decide he was worth a try, and came over. She stood beside him at the bar and put her hand on his arm. 'You going to buy me a drink, then?'

Up close, his first impression became certain knowledge. She was as young, blonde and pretty as a dozen other girls he saw every day, and had a third dimension that was far too familiar to desire – he found it easy to imagine that her thin gold necklace had been bought by a fiancé or a sister, that she lived with her parents in a house much like his own. 'I'm Vicki,' she said. 'I've seen you in here before.'

'Yeah.' He didn't want to talk to her, but couldn't think of any way not to. 'Suppose you have.'

'You never stay long, do you? How come you always run off so fast?'

He was in the wrong, he realised suddenly, just for standing in this club, talking to this girl. He thought of Marie at home, making a start on the dinner. 'I have to. I'm married.'

'That supposed to shock me or something?' She giggled, not quite contemptuously. 'So's every man comes in here, darlin'. I won't tell if you don't.'

The lights from the glittering disco globe spun faster across the bar, and the music grew louder. The girl's hoop earrings glinted red, and a red light caught tiny points in her pale eyes. For a second, Terry thought she looked different and unplaceably exciting – her face was bony, watchful, shadowed with the decadent liberty he'd come in search of. Unnerved by the suddenness of the attraction, he spoke harshly, pushing her away in his mind and embracing Marie. 'I'm not like the others. I love my wife. *I love my wife.*'

The girl sounded alarmed, nakedly contemptuous now. 'All right. Keep your hair on. I only *said.*' She took a step away from him, and he felt her allure crumble – the too-good necklace, the perfume he could almost have named, the tattoo on the shoulder that implied a life beyond here. 'If you're not going to buy me a drink, I can't stand here,' she said. 'We can get fired for just chatting.'

'You're wasting your time,' he said, not unkindly. 'Go on. You'll meet someone else. Make some money.'

'Hardly anyone else in here yet.' But she went, obviously irritated at having wasted her time. More girls had arrived while they'd been talking, and he watched her return to the four or five who now sat smoking at a table. Their mouths moved inaudibly beneath the music, as behind thick glass, and he wondered if they were talking about him. Something in the sight pierced him with an indefinable loneliness. He was an alien here – but part of him yearned for this darkness, although the long, quiet hours in the indifferent office had stamped him for life. He stood and sipped, and gazed at the dancer like an exile.

The voice across the bar took him by surprise. 'Would you like another drink, sir?'

'Better not.' It was getting busier, he saw. The girls were drifting up from the table as besuited men came through the red-velvet curtains; the music pounded, the lights spun. 'Time

I went home, I think.' And he smiled, put down his empty glass and turned away, full of the sneaking disappointment he'd come to associate with leaving this place, going home.

He was half-way up the stairs when he saw her. She was hurrying down, and the light caught red in her coal-black hair. For a second, they glanced at each other. He had a second's impression of dark, unfathomable loveliness – red lips gleaming like fresh paint, long white hand rising to brush hair from cold blue eyes – and then she was hurrying down the stairs again, and the moment was gone.

4

He's looking at you, whispered Christine, in Rosina's mind. *Everyone always looks at you, Rosina.*

But Rosina ignored the voice as she always did. She was very nearly late, and they noticed in here if you often came in late. She'd known for a long time that it paid to keep the little rules that didn't really matter.

She passed most of the other girls talking round the bar as she headed for the toilets-cum-dressing-rooms, catching a dozen random snippets of conversation through the music. Noise hammered and ricocheted in her mind, and blocked out anything Christine might have to say. It was a relief. She didn't have anything in common with Christine any more, and wasn't sure why the memory of her kept coming back.

Inside, the dressing room was almost deserted, and the heavy silence was underscored by the buzzing striplights. Vicki stood alone, adjusting her hair in front of a mirror.

'All right, Rosina?' she asked, smiling, turning. 'How's it going?'

'I'm fine.' Rosina always came to work ready-dressed in her evening clothes, and had only to reapply makeup in here. She extracted red lipstick, black eyebrow-pencil and kohl from her bag, set them down on the counter. 'How are you?'

'Not so bad.' Vicki frowned at herself in the mirror, then at the girl beside her. 'That bloke was in here earlier. I spoke to him.'

'What bloke?'

'You know,' said Vicki, 'or maybe you don't. You're never here when he comes in. He's always early.'

Rosina leaned closer to the mirror, raised the kohl pencil, drew thick black lines round her eyes. '*What* bloke?'

'A gorgeous one. Weird, though. Went on about how much he loved his wife.' Vicki yawned theatrically, giggled. 'Never sits down with anyone. Fucking gorgeous, though, I tell you.'

'What does he look like?'

'Blond hair. Almost white.' Vicki finished with the hair-brush and replaced it in her bag. 'You'd know him if you'd seen him.'

'I think I did see him.' Rosina watched herself in the mirror – it was as if she was talking to herself. 'On the stairs.'

'Gorgeous,' said Vicki. She turned away. 'See you later, anyway. It's busy tonight.'

When the door had wheezed shut behind the other girl, Rosina watched herself in the mirror for a few minutes longer. The disco noise was tiny in the background as Christine watched her from the glass. Perhaps she didn't mind Christine being here after all, she thought, because there was something both soothing and thrilling about the awe in Christine's imagined eyes, and the way that Christine was always afraid made her enjoy her own recklessness all the more.

You're not afraid of anything, Rosina, murmured Christine. *I wish I was you . . .*

5

Terry was reminded of all the things he most wanted to forget as soon as he'd gone through the ticket barriers at Oxford Circus underground station and stepped on to the escalator leading down. Three or four posters he didn't recognise saluted him briefly, giving way to one he knew immediately. A bizarre photographic image of a City gent riding a shark underwater, a headline that leaped out and nailed you right in the brain. *Try something new.* An ad that got noticed, remembered.

That's Rob and Christian's work, Terry. Of course.

He didn't hate Rob and Christian, he told himself. They were nice boys, in their loud, laddish way, good-natured, easy to get along with. It wasn't their fault that they were in their early twenties and already the unquestioned stars of the advertising agency he worked at, that they were obviously moving on to bigger and better things in the near future and the creative director thought the sun rose and fell on them. But they reminded him painfully of too much – the way his knowledge of his failure robbed him of the confidence to speak up in meetings, the patronising tone in which the creative director spoke to him, the way his colleagues had written him off long ago. And that in turn was bound up with too much else, stirred dark emotions that he knew Rob and Christian would never understand. Failure was a loaded word for him, and extended into areas that had nothing to do with work.

Failure, doubt and fear. In his mind, they were one and the same, and the little voice he didn't want to hear expressed them all too vividly. These days, only Marie still believed in him – in his intelligence and potential – and her belief was becoming worse than anything, reminding him of what else he was concealing from her. He'd become terrified that she'd discover the secrets of his life along with his failure – they seemed to run in tandem, the vast and the trivial, the things that would drive her away.

Recently it had all been escalating. The doubts and fears he'd been blocking out for twenty-five years feeding off his increasing unimportance in the office, and growing at an appalling speed . . . the unsettling little voice he'd first heard as a child becoming harder and harder to ignore . . .

On the tube, he sat and looked out of the window at the black tunnel walls and the reflected interior of the carriage, and was overcome by a tidal wave of longing. He thought about a gleaming red mouth seen under thin rosy lights, about something remote, enigmatic and icily sensual that had never been afraid as he was now. It was as if the girl he'd seen moved a little further away from him with every second that passed. She had belonged to the amoral and anonymous night, he thought, and then remembered Marie, who suspected nothing, and the son they'd never have together, and the memory of the black-haired girl moved inside him like music.

Then he got off the tube, ascended the escalator and emerged into the railway station proper. He boarded the train to Streatham Hill and waited for home to arrive.

6

Over the past few months, Marie had been fighting off a vague suspicion that Terry was having an affair. There was, she knew, no real basis for the suspicion – no mysterious phone calls or crumpled notes encountered in the pockets while she was washing clothes, no marked increase or decrease in their sex-life. But there was no denying that he had been in a strange mood lately, and while she'd have liked to put it all down to his father's death, she found that she couldn't. She'd spent enough time with Terry and his father to know that they'd never been close – in each other's company, the two men had acted like polite, distant acquaintances. Besides, it had begun well before his father's death – as much as a month before.

Now they sat in the kitchen together, eating dinner, and she couldn't hold back her news any longer. She'd wanted him to notice her half-feigned happiness and ask her about it, but he'd sat and eaten in silence, and hadn't seemed to notice anything.

'Guess what happened at work today?'

He glanced up with distracted eyes. 'What?'

'I got promoted,' she said, with deliberate brightness. 'I'm the new head of Credit. Found out this afternoon.'

'You're joking.'

'Cross my heart, I'm not.' His sudden animation pleased her. She carried on quickly, 'The managing director called me into his office. Asked me if I'd like to accept. Like I was going to say no.'

'God,' he said slowly. 'Well done.'

'And you won't believe how much better the money is, Terry,' she said. 'They're putting me up to *forty grand a year*.'

For a long, slow second, he just looked at her, fork half-way to his mouth. 'Bloody hell, Marie. That's a jump of—'

'Twelve grand. Tell me about it.' It had seemed incredible at the time, but now that the news had sunk in, it felt like no more than a simple fact. 'We might be able to go away for Christmas, after all.'

Away from here, she wanted to say, *away from this strange mood of yours, to where we could get things back to normal.* But he seemed not to pick up on the subtext, and spoke quietly. 'You'll be earning more than me.'

The stricken look in his eyes made her take a step back inside – she remembered the night before last, when she'd woken up and he hadn't been beside her. 'It doesn't bother you, does it, Terry? There's no reason why it should.'

'I know. It's all right. I'm pleased for you,' he said. 'We should have a glass of wine to celebrate.'

He got a bottle out of the fridge, uncorked it and poured two glasses in silence. It was a disturbing travesty of a celebration, she thought, his preoccupation was almost palpable. '*Terry.*'

'What?'

He set down the glasses on the table and looked at her. She realised she couldn't put her unease into words. 'Nothing,' she said. 'By the way, I spoke to Allie earlier. She's got one of her gigs this weekend. I said we'd have Lisa again.'

His shoulders rose and fell and he said nothing. She felt an overwhelming need to kick-start his apathy. 'You don't mind, do you? She's a nice kid. Never any trouble.'

'Of course I don't mind. You know I like having her around.' They sat and ate, and sipped at their wine for a while. 'Anyway, congratulations,' he said eventually. 'I've got some work to be getting on with, I'm afraid. I'll be in the study.'

'You shouldn't bring so much back with you,' she said. 'You'll wear yourself out.'

His only answer was a small rueful smile that seemed inexplicably evasive. He rose from the table and left the room.

Alone in the warm, well-lit chrome and pinewood kitchen, Marie raised her glass and sipped. Pathos threatened to overwhelm her. Happy promotion, Marie, she thought. He'd congratulated her, but he *hadn't* congratulated her: three months ago they'd have shared a celebratory dinner together in the living room, but now he'd escaped to his study like an animal seeking out its den.

7

It was unquestionably *his* study, although the rest of the pleasant Streatham Hill terrace was theirs. In some way she couldn't quite understand, he had adopted the little room at the back of the house, with its desk and computer and bookshelf and not much else. During the last few weeks, he'd spent much of his time there, and Marie had no idea what he was doing.

Well, of course she knew he was working. That was what he always told her. *I've had to bring some work home with me, I'm afraid. I've got some things to get done by tomorrow.* But while there was nothing suspicious about that *per se*, she couldn't help noticing that his increased workload had coincided exactly with his withdrawn mood, couldn't help wondering whether the mood led him to invent more work than he actually had, just so he could shut himself away from her.

It wasn't like Terry to get wound up over pressure at work. In the early days of their marriage, he'd thrived on it – and he'd never been known to bring anything home *then*.

And there was no sound of typing when he was shut away in the study, these days. There was never any sound at all.

Marie washed up and went into the living room, where she put the telly on to banish the uncomfortable silence of the study. She wished she could conjure some mental image of Terry reading work documents or writing brochure copy in longhand. But she couldn't envisage him doing anything whatsoever. It unsettled her more than a little: they were separated by no more than two walls, and he might as well have been in a foreign country.

And if she broke the habit of a lifetime by forcing a direct confrontation, asked him what the hell he *did* in there, she knew the answer would come straight back at her like a thrown ball: *I was working. Of course I was working, Marie . . .*

The night before last, she'd woken up in the middle of the night – the clock-radio by the bed had told her it had just gone half two. She'd reached out sleepily to touch him, but her hand had met nothing except empty sheets. At first she'd thought he must be in the bathroom, but there was no sound from there. There was no sound from anywhere in the house. Although he wasn't in the habit of making himself late-night snacks, she assumed he must be in the kitchen, and waited ten minutes for him to come back to bed. He didn't. Suddenly wide awake, she tiptoed downstairs without knowing quite why.

But the kitchen was dark, and the living room was dark, and the hallway was illuminated by nothing but moonlight. The only artificial light was a thin rectangle round the closed study door. And the silence was absolute.

Was he really *working* at a quarter to three in the morning?

Telling herself he wouldn't want to be disturbed, she'd tiptoed back up the stairs, more than ever desperate not to be heard. It was odd how quickly exhaustion had overcome uneasiness in bed. By ten past four she was asleep again, and when she'd woken up in the morning, he'd been right there beside her. As if he'd never been away.

She sat in the living room and watched TV, trying her utmost to forget about that night. Maybe he'd remembered something that needed to be done by the morning, she told herself. There were any number of possible explanations. But as she went over them in her mind, none felt right somehow, and she felt unable to demand an explanation from him. It seemed a very long time before Terry came out of the study and into the living room, and they watched a little more TV together before turning in for the night.

8

He couldn't sleep. It was almost half past one, and he couldn't sleep.

Maybe that's what's wrong with you, Terry. Just plain old-fashioned exhaustion . . .

For once, however, he knew that the little voice was wrong: the sleeplessness was a symptom, not a cause. Part of him wanted to go back down to the study, but he knew he couldn't. If he did that too often, Marie might wake up and find him gone – might even come downstairs and surprise him there. And if she did that, she might discover—

Discover what, Terry?

Suddenly he pictured the child he and Marie couldn't have – a boy of slim build and average height, whose colouring was saved from the realms of albino by a single shade and a half. A quiet, guarded little boy who tried far too hard to seem contented. A beautiful little boy, passing adults would say. But he could give his son far more than cold-eyed compliments that meant nothing. He could make his son grow up feeling loved.

An image rose in his mind of that little boy sitting in a sun-drenched vicarage kitchen, trying not to fidget, listening to the quick staccato of grown-ups' voices around him. *So this is Terry,* they said, *what a beautiful little boy. And this must be Katie. Aah. Come here, sweetheart . . .*

His sister, four years his junior. Sweet little Katie. In the early days, he'd watched her without envy, with the fascination you felt for another species. How effortlessly happy and vivacious she was, how fearlessly in love with the world. She was as plump and pretty as a cherub, and her colouring was as vivid as his own would never be – golden curls, bright blue eyes, rosy cheeks. An adorable child. He'd adored her at first, just as everyone else did, because she was his little sister, and he could help protect her from the world.

The Fielding children. What a happy, sheltered, idyllic childhood they'd shared. Their father, the vicar, cheerful, jovial, well-liked by everyone in the parish. Their crisp, efficient mother, effortlessly elegant in knitwear and tweeds, who organised church fairs like clockwork and had a seat on the PTA. The big old red-brick vicarage they called home, with veins of ivy twining up the walls, and a sloping back garden that led on to an orchard rich with shiny red apples. Two happy, well-fed, photogenic children, growing up in an environment of security and love . . .

It was how the people around him had seen his early life, and how he knew Marie saw it now. And even though he knew how false the picture was, part of Terry couldn't help wanting to believe in it. It would have been wonderful to have had a childhood like that. A childhood with no dark secrets.

Little Katie lying dead in the apple orchard. The stark moment of horror as he looked down at her and realised why she'd been killed.

You wouldn't have had to know things like that, he thought. *I'd have kept you safe from them,* and realised he was talking in his mind to a son who would never exist. He'd never get the chance to step back in time and mould a different version of himself and his past, not now, not ever.

He lay back and closed his eyes, and tried to stop himself thinking about the past. It was over now. Both his parents were dead, just as Katie was. His life now and his life then had nothing to do with one another.

Sleep drifted in slowly. On the outskirts of oblivion, he saw a pale-haired little boy, and heard Katie's happy gurgling laughter turn up louder and louder, echoing through the darkness around him with the power of a nightmare.

9

'I can't thank you enough for taking her this weekend, Marie,' said Allie, setting a cup of tea by Marie's hand. 'I don't like to ask Mum, really, not at her age. And it'd be a shame if I had to give up my career just when it's taking off.'

While Allie's one-bedroomed flat was among the smallest Marie had ever seen, she found it an immensely pleasant place to spend time in – all bright primary colours and fresh-looking white paint, a touch of the nursery and *Changing Rooms* both at once. Allie had a way with surroundings. Sitting in the armchair by the gas-fire, Marie sipped her tea. 'How's it going, your singing?'

Allie's face lit up. 'Fantastic. I'm getting bookings for every weekend. Doing Pontin's in Weymouth tonight and tomorrow. A club up West on Wednesday – don't worry, I'm getting a babysitter for *that.* And I'm up for a gig on a cruise ship next year.'

At twenty-nine, Marie thought, Allie still had *little sister* written all over her. There was something inescapably teenage in her bleached-blonde hair and yellow-painted nails, her undiscriminating enthusiasm for her favourite things. The two of them shared nothing but a certain vivacity of manner, and facial similarities that the casual eye would have missed: the wide spacing of the eyes, the slight dimples that showed with a broad smile. 'Glad to hear it's going well,' said Marie. 'I know it upset you a bit when you had to give it up.'

'Wouldn't have had it any other way,' said Allie promptly. 'Not while Lise was a little kid and all. But, you know, now she's almost seven. You don't mind staying with your auntie some weekends, do you, Lise?'

The affectionate diminutive was addressed to the door. Marie looked round to see that Lisa had just walked into the room. She was a slight, pale, pretty child, with long straight hair of a sandy-beige colour and huge grey eyes. The resemblance between mother and daughter was intense. 'You know I don't, Mum.'

'That's the girl.' Allie smiled at her as Marie did. Lisa picked up a hair-ruffle from a corner table, and left the room. 'It'll be in her best interests and all, you know,' Allie continued blithely. 'I mean, you only hear about Britney Spears and Billie Piper and all the teenagers, but a singer's life doesn't *have* to end at twenty-five. Look at Macy Gray. And Jane McDonald.'

'You've got a point.' Privately, Marie doubted that her sister would ever get a record deal, never mind a top-ten hit, but she supposed that stranger things had happened. 'It could change your lives.'

'Wouldn't have to get her school things second-hand then, I can tell you,' said Allie wistfully. She lowered her voice: 'I try my best not to slag Tony off to Lise, but I could kill that bastard sometimes. What sort of man just runs off when his daughter's a year old, and leaves his girlfriend to carry the can?'

There was no answer to that. Marie sighed. 'You know, I'm happy to lend you some money, Allie. It's not fair on you, having to struggle like this.'

'Keep it. Really. I'm all right. Probably exaggerated a bit.' Allie's slender shoulders rose and fell in a quick, reflexive gesture. 'Dad sent me a couple of hundred the other week, you know. Along with the usual lectures.'

'He doesn't mean any harm.' A brief shared image flashed between them; a neat little house in Bromley, a kindly, old-fashioned, rather repressive couple who'd been in their fifties when their daughters were in their teens. They still hadn't quite got used to the idea of a single mother in the family. 'Poor old Dad. Don't mind him, Allie.'

'I'll try not to.' Allie's wistful moods never lasted longer than her moments of irritation. Already she was back to cheerful irresponsibility, irrepressible optimism. 'Well, suppose you and Lise had better get going, hadn't you?'

Marie called Lisa from the bedroom, they said goodbye and Allie said she'd be round first thing Monday morning to pick Lisa up. After that, there was nothing to do but leave.

After the warmth of Allie's flat, the day outside was punishingly cold. Marie walked hand in hand with Lisa, heading home, her worries about Terry like an unreachable itch at the back of her mind.

10

Terry had never felt comfortable with Allie, or Lisa, or Marie's parents. Even during the good days, he had been frightened by the idea that Marie had a life away from him, had other deep attachments that maybe meant more to her than he did. He didn't understand why it should matter to him – he'd never thought of himself as a possessive or a jealous husband – but somehow it mattered far too much. It was what had made him fall in love with Marie and what had kept him faithful to her for the last ten years: the idea that she loved him more than anyone, that he had the first and most important claim on her optimism and her laughter.

You have to lie to keep that love now, Terry. If she sees how afraid you really are – and why – it's going to be gone in a second . . .

It was half one on Sunday afternoon, and he, Marie and Lisa were walking up Streatham Hill towards the cinema. Recently, Lisa's presence unnerved him – the huge grey eyes that seemed to look straight at everything he was in the most agony to hide, at the lies he'd been forced to tell and the lies he'd sought out for reasons he didn't understand. *My father didn't have anything to leave in his will,* he'd said to Marie two weeks ago. *I was as surprised as anyone.* Perhaps the cold unblinking judgement was all in his own mind, and not in his niece at all. Still, the way she looked at him sometimes put him on edge.

'Where shall we go after the film?' asked Marie, as she walked, holding Lisa's hand. 'For a late pub lunch, or—'

'That's a good idea,' he said, with a brightness he hoped matched hers. 'Whatever.'

He tried to taste a family man's contentment, but by the time they were entering the cinema, doubts and creeping fears were gnawing at his mind. That night, he'd lie awake and remember Katie; the following morning, he'd go into the office and laugh along with people who ignored him. It all seemed to be the same thing, somehow, disparate symptoms of the same terminal disease. They bought popcorn and plastic cups of Diet Coke and Fanta, and went into Screen Three, and sat down.

The film wasn't anything in particular, but he lost his fears for an hour or so in a fast-moving vivacity that took him away from the truth of himself – perky, meaningless choruses, carefully choreographed dancing animals, a happy ending he could have written in advance. After the credits had rolled,

Lisa enthused about it all the way out of the cinema. 'And it was brilliant when he chased the monkey up the tree,' she babbled, 'and when they went into the castle and . . .'

Marie questioned her, agreed, humoured her. Looking at his wife, Terry felt his anxiety return, because she seemed as happy as she ever did alone with him, and it hurt him to see her as cheerful and vivacious with someone else. *I thought you loved me best*, he thought, in confusion, and an image of his mother flashed hard behind his eyes – cold, indifferent, Julia Fielding, whose good opinion he'd longed for, who'd only ever smiled at his sister.

There was a pub a few doors down from the cinema, and they went for lunch in there. After the chilly afternoon, which was already getting dark, its interior was warm, welcoming and comfortable, bright with colourful blackboards and strangers' chatter. They found a table by the window and studied the menus. 'It's nice in here, isn't it?' said Marie. 'The food looks great, too.'

'Can I have scampi?' asked Lisa.

'Sure.' Terry fought for bonhomie and ease of manner, but the cool grey six-year-old eyes terrified him. *It's not your imagination, Terry*, the voice said. *She really can see what you're hiding*. Out of nowhere, he felt on the brink of a full-blown panic attack, and knew he had to get away before Marie noticed. 'Be back in a minute,' he said, smiling as he rose from the table. 'Just going to the loo.'

Terry walked through the double doors that led on to the gents', his heart thumping hard in his chest. A narrow passage was lined with framed movie posters, and his footsteps echoed nightmarishly along it. At the end, a second set of doors stood propped open by beer barrels, facing on to a deserted patio. White plastic tables gleamed in the deepening dusk, and the floodlit glow was yellow and eerie.

He stood gazing out there for a long time, collecting his thoughts, forcing the voice back, calming his rush of fear with cold fresh air and solitude. He realised he was thinking about the black-haired girl from the club. How white her skin had been, he remembered. How red her lips.

11

'Read me another chapter, Auntie Marie,' Lisa said, as Marie closed the book.

'No, Lise. It's time you were asleep.' Marie rose from the bed. 'Your mum'll be round to fetch you first thing in the morning.'

In bed, Lisa watched her. 'What was she singing tonight?'

'Now, how should I know that?' Marie smiled. 'You'll have to ask her tomorrow.'

'I will,' said Lisa absently, then curled up and fell asleep.

Marie reached out and switched off the side-lamp.

Downstairs, Terry was in the living room watching telly. She sat on the sofa beside him, trying to forget his strangeness and talk to him as she'd used to.

'She's gone to sleep already, little love.'

For some time, he didn't speak, and his eyes stayed fixed on the screen. Her worries, forgotten while she'd been alone with Lisa, rushed back into her mind like fast-flowing water. She hated confrontation, but now it was the only way to go on. 'Terry, what's the matter?'

He turned to look at her. 'What do you mean?'

'Oh, come on, you know exactly what I mean. You've hardly said a word all weekend.'

'It's just work, Marie. I'm . . . a bit preoccupied. I'm sorry.' He took a long, deep breath. 'Look, I've got some things to get on with. I won't be long.'

Exasperation overcame her, oddly mundane in the midst of her growing unease. She spoke sharply. 'Let me guess. In the study.'

'Of course in the study, Marie. Where else?'

'Oh, of *course.* Where else have you been in the evenings lately?' Confusion made her angry – anger made her shrewish. 'What do you do in there? I never hear typing. I never hear *anything.*'

'I write copy. Longhand. I type it up at work.' In an instant, he was chilly and defensive – he spoke as if she'd insulted him. 'What do you think I'm doing in there? Jerking off?'

'Of course not. Don't be so ridiculous—' but he was rising from his seat and walking out of the room. Alone on the sofa, she changed the TV channel and sighed. Less than a week ago she'd suspected he might be having an affair but now she was convinced that there was even more to it than that. There was something almost morbid in his need for solitude and silence – something secretive and obsessive.

He didn't act like a man in the early stages of an affair. He acted like a man in the early stages of a breakdown . . .

She remembered how it had been six years ago, when their attempts at starting a family had gone on for too long, when they'd finally acknowledged something was wrong and had gone to a doctor. How he'd reacted when the doctor had broken the news of his infertility. In the surgery, he'd been silent and shell-shocked – but later that night . . .

She'd been tentative, sympathetic, moved by his beaten silence in the living room. At first, she'd kept a tactful distance, but something about his demeanour gradually demanded more eloquent reassurance. 'It's all right, Terry,' she'd said, coming out of the kitchen, 'you know it doesn't matter to me,' and she'd put the cup of tea she'd just made beside his hand, which was as pale and umoving as the hand of a waxwork.

And then he'd lashed out. Sent the tea spinning from the table in a wild splash of brownish liquid to smash against the wall, and he'd stood up. Her cautious sympathy had snapped into horror in the blink of an eye. Terry didn't have a temper – he'd never had a temper—

'It matters to *me!*' he'd yelled, and his eyes had been shining with tears and a look that was almost insanity. 'You don't understand. You just don't understand how it feels,' and then he'd stormed out of the room, and the study door had slammed hard behind him.

And it had been impossible, unthinkable, that normal service could resume straight away after something like that, but it had. She'd gone to bed and lain sleepless for a long time before exhaustion knocked her out. Then when she'd woken in the morning, he'd been there beside her as always, and his only reference to last night's outburst had been so normal, so wildly out of proportion to the horror she remembered, that she began to think maybe she'd exaggerated it in her mind . . .

'I'm really sorry I snapped at you last night, Marie. That news . . . came as quite a blow . . .'

She hadn't asked further. She'd been far too relieved. More than anything, she wanted to believe his version of last night – he'd taken a bad blow and he'd *snapped* at her and, anyway, no harm had been done. As the weeks passed, the last of her reservations faded, and she saw him almost exactly as she had before – a nice, easy-going man who didn't have a temper, a gorgeous, pleasant and reliable husband she was lucky to have. All he'd done was *snap* at her. Once.

She thought he'd be keen to try artificial insemination, or adoption, or fostering, but to her surprise, his indifference couldn't have been greater. While she didn't mind herself – she'd never been that keen on the idea of kids – she couldn't help but be curious as to why he'd apparently stopped caring about being a father. One evening curiosity had overcome an apprehension to which she stubbornly refused to put a name, and she'd asked him outright. She dreaded a second outburst, but he couldn't have seemed calmer. He just looked at her, and smiled regretfully: 'It wouldn't be the same, Marie, having a child that wasn't *ours*.'

What the hell was he doing in that study? she wondered. Sitting in the living room and remembering that isolated outburst had disturbed her – she wanted to see him and talk to him, remember that he wasn't a psycho or a madman, but just a preoccupied husband who'd brought a lot of work home recently. She got up from the sofa, walked out into the hallway and rapped on the study door. 'Terry.'

'Just a second.'

Did he sound strained, startled? Of course, she thought, her knock had taken him by surprise – but that note in his voice seemed to imply something close to fear of discovery. There was a tiny muffled noise that might have been a drawer slamming shut – that might have been anything.

'Come in.'

She opened the door and stepped inside. He was sitting at an empty patch of desk beside the computer. The screen showed only black, and there was nothing on the desk but a pad of blank white paper.

'You've been in here ages,' she said. 'Come into the living room. There's that Woody Allen film starting in ten minutes.'

'All right. I'll be out soon.'

She smiled and went back to the living room. But she didn't feel like smiling. He didn't seem to realise what he'd just betrayed to her, but that quickly cleared desk had told its own story. Whatever he did in that study was something he didn't want her to know about, and she'd have bet a month's salary that it had nothing to do with work.

12

The time was edging slowly past midnight, and – in an Escape-scented room with black walls – Rosina was having a strange dream. In it, she was watching scenes from the past on a television screen. Two girls entering a house. It was strange, unnerving, to see yourself and someone you'd once known so well as if you were both acting.

The two girls looked around sixteen. One was strikingly lovely, with long straight dark hair, pale skin and an air of leadership. The other was more ordinary, a pretty, baby-faced blonde who moved and spoke diffidently.

Love your house, Rosina, said the blonde.

The dark girl ignored her. *Come on,* she said, closing the door. *Come on up to my room. I've got something to tell you.*

Inside, the house was large, airy, impeccably decorated. The camera closed in on a silver-framed photograph on a table-top, and stayed with it for long, slow seconds. It showed a middle-aged man and woman in evening dress, the woman sequined, the man crisp black and white. He was grey-haired and heavy-set, and he smiled at the camera with the easy assurance of prosperity. The woman was beautiful, and her resemblance to the dark girl was unmistakable.

Then the camera turned away to follow the girls' backs up the last few stairs, and into a bedroom as pretty as a wedding-cake, where the immediate impression was of white lace and pale pinewood.

Love your room, Rosina, said the blonde girl.

The dark girl shrugged. There was something both compelling and disturbing about her – a coldness in the eyes, a chilly precision in her voice when she spoke. *Can you keep a secret, Christine?*

Course I can. The blonde girl spoke quickly, eagerly. *You know I can.*

Do you want to help me get back at someone?

Who is it?

Does it matter? The dark girl laughed, and the laugh both jarred with and complemented the rest of her – a child's laugh, unselfconscious. *Either you're going to help me or you're not.*

A brief, edgy silence fell, and the camera wandered round the room, as though an unseen director was marvelling at everything as the blonde girl did. A well-manicured little townhouse garden through the bay window, wardrobe doors standing tantalisingly shut, a letter on the dressing table addressed to Miss R. Parker. Then it returned to the action, the blonde girl looking apprehensive, but nodding just the same. *Course I will, Rosina.*

Good. I knew you would.

Another tense silence, this one shorter. When the blonde girl spoke, it was as if she was steeling herself to face the inevitable. *Who is it?*

Mrs Martin, said the dark girl, and the camera closed in for one last time on the blonde girl's frightened eyes, and it was then that Rosina woke up.

13

It was strange how the black-haired girl's image gripped Terry more deeply with each day that passed. It was like watching a burn form. When he'd first seen her on the stairs of the club he'd had no idea that she'd infected him like this, but now, three days later, he saw a darting image of her every time he closed his eyes. A girl who looked like a beautiful vampire, who'd never known this paranoia and despair, who'd never sat drinking strong black coffee in a bright well-decorated pinewood kitchen, feeling the subtle terror of another Monday at work moving closer.

'That'll be Allie,' said Marie, as the doorbell rang. 'You got everything, Lise?'

Lisa nodded indifferently, eyes downcast. 'Mmm.'

Terry watched Marie get up to answer the door, and a sense of inevitability took hold of him. These days, Allie's arrival always marked the beginning of his week at work, the too-long, too-brief journey that would end in a seventh-floor boardroom in Soho Square. The creative director had instigated the Monday-morning meetings three weeks ago, immediately after they'd moved to their new offices. 'Well, suppose I'd better be off,' he said, with hollow joviality, smiling goodbye to Lisa as Marie and Allie came into the kitchen. 'See you later, Marie. 'Bye, Allie.' And then home was ending, and he was putting on his coat in the hallway, walking out into the cold.

He had been dreading the too-familiar journey all weekend, but imagining it in advance did nothing to diminish its power over him. The anguish always came fresh to him. At Streatham Hill station, he boarded the train like a condemned man heading for the appointed place of execution, knowing there was nothing left for him but a boardroom full of eyes that looked straight through him – and Rodge, the nearest thing he had to a friend there, who despised him just as much as everyone else.

Just like school, isn't it, Terry? When you were a child . . .

How closely his days in the office were linked to the things that really mattered – the little voice in his mind that never went away now, what he looked at in the study when he needed to be alone. Failure and insignificance travelled hand in hand with meaningless moments of admiration – the female account handlers who stared at him in the office and the adults who had said, *What a beautiful little boy* – and images that mattered far too much. An orchard rich with shiny red apples. Little Katie.

So why don't you just switch jobs, Terry? Copywriting's not the only career in the world – and even if it was, there are other agencies in London . . .

But he knew perfectly well that there was no point in even thinking about it. Copywriting was all he knew how to do at all well, and any other agency would treat him just the same. If they offered him a job at all. He was thirty-seven, an old man in an industry dominated by twenty-three-year-olds, and he hadn't produced anything exceptional in years. For the sake of the meagre monthly payslip, he was trapped.

But what about your father dying, Terry? What about the secret you didn't share with your wife?

He forced himself to cut off the voice. The simple fact was, he didn't know why he was doing what he did. And he didn't much like to think about that. He'd done things for reasons he hadn't understood once before in his life, and – alone in the study in the evenings – he remembered far too vividly what *that* had led to.

No, he told himself, there was no way out now.

At Victoria station, he moved in a tide of blank-eyed strangers down to the Underground. He went through the ticket barriers and stepped on to the escalator, feeling the seventh-floor boardroom move inexorably closer.

14

Rob and Christian were twenty-two and twenty-three respectively, and always reminded Terry of young male singer-songwriters he and Marie had seen interviewed on chat shows – as if, when you passed a certain level of talent, greasy hair and dirty trainers became status-symbols. When he walked into the bleak seventh-floor boardroom, Rob was sitting with his feet on the table and Christian was smoking a cigarette, and they were talking in the middle of the little group of sycophants that seemed to have coalesced around them.

'Had a fucking hangover on Sunday,' Rob was complaining. 'Went to Ministry and got shitfaced. Drank so much I couldn't hardly stand up, never mind anything else.'

'You sure drinking was all you got up to?' asked Christian slyly. 'You weren't under the influence of anything else?' and they and the group around them burst out laughing. It was a harsh, jagged sound that seemed to scrape at the inside of Terry's skull as he took a seat beside them. 'Listening to the Chemical Brothers, were you?' and the laughter rang out again, locking Terry out.

From the corner of his eye, he saw Rodge come in, a short chubby man of around thirty-five, whose leather jacket and ponytail weren't fooling anyone. He sat beside Terry, and as always, greeted Rob and Christian first. 'All right, lads?' he called out jovially. 'Have a good weekend?' They looked round and muttered something good-natured before returning to tales of weekend drunkenness and one-night stands. Rodge turned back to Terry with an air of half-amiable, half-contemptuous disappointment. 'All right, Terry?'

'Yeah.' Terry's despair intensified – he realised he was grateful to Rodge for talking to him. 'You?'

'Not bad. Went on a pub-crawl on Saturday night. Got very, very drunk.' It was like a bad parody of the way Rob and Christian spoke – Rodge's puffy little eyes darted over to them constantly. 'You remember what it's like when you're young, Terry. You just don't care.'

Rodge always spoke as if Terry was ten rather than two years older than him, but Terry couldn't bring himself to dislike him. His motives were too obvious and too sad to dislike, and Terry could see his own fear of redundancy reflected too clearly in Rodge's eyes. 'You'll settle down,' he said, with cynical humour, 'when you get to my age,' and then the creative director came in, and the room fell quiet.

'Top of the morning to you, boys and girls,' said Viv Sacker chummily. 'Now, let's get down to the order of the day.'

Only in Sacker's position, Terry thought, did age stop mattering in a creative department. Sacker was a tall, thin man somewhere in his forties with an electric shock of curly black hair, a fraying tweed jacket that had become his permanent trademark, and an outstanding copywriting career that extended behind him like an aristocrat's family tree. He had cold eyes above a wide smile, and used the word 'young' as a committed Nazi might have used 'Aryan'.

'And as you all know,' he was saying, 'we're moving towards a whole new culture here, a fresh, young, dynamic culture. I'm hoping we'll do well at the awards next week. Our young stars here have three campaigns entered and, I must say, I'm pinning my hopes on a major triumph.'

If only Sacker had been talking about him, Terry thought, with an agonising stab of something far beyond jealousy. He watched Rob and Christian exchange bored, self-conscious smiles that didn't even care enough to be smug, watched Christian light yet another Marlboro. It was like looking back to a happy, unreachable past through locked iron gates – the major industry award he'd won at the age of twenty-eight and the promise of a glittering future, the relief and dizzy joy of having finally escaped dark dreams and creeping terrors. But they'd only been hiding, lying in wait for insignificance to return. 'So let's keep our fingers crossed for next Friday night at the Grosvenor House,' Sacker was saying. 'Of course, we won't all get to go, but I'll try to get our department as many tickets as humanly possible.'

Terry knew that Rob and Christian and a couple of their cronies would get tickets, while he and Rodge wouldn't in a million years. He was gripped by a sense of tragedy that expanded to block out the world. After work, he thought, he'd go to the club and seek out the black-haired girl. This morning, the club and the black-haired girl were the only things he had to pin his hopes on.

15

'So how's the new job going?'

Marie and Sandra were sitting in Pizza Express up the road from their office, eating lunch. It was a bright, chilly winter day, and dazzling sunlight caught a nearby window. The restaurant was crowded, the noise from other people's conversations a steady, muted roar, underscored by the click of forks on plates, glass on glass, little sounds of a busy London lunchtime.

'Too early to say, really. I've only been in Martin's old office a few hours.'

Marie had moved her things in this morning – her pens and stress-relief toys, and the framed snapshot of Terry she always kept by her computer. It didn't feel quite like her office yet, though. 'Get up to anything over the weekend?'

'Just stayed at home with Derek and the kids, really. How about you?'

'Me and Terry were babysitting my little niece. Went to see *Dinosaur*, of all things,' said Marie. 'I'm getting a bit worried about Terry, Sandra. He doesn't seem quite himself.'

'How do you mean?'

'I don't know. It's hard to say.' She remembered the dead black computer screen and the empty desk, the sound of a drawer closing when she'd knocked on the study door. It seemed impossible to describe now: chilly sunlight and lunchtime crowds made her worries seem paranoid and formless. 'He just seems . . . distant. A bit withdrawn.'

'Probably still upset about his dad,' said Sandra sagely. 'Takes time to get over a parent dying.'

'I know. That's probably what it is.' But it was a routine, knee-jerk response, and she knew it – she'd thrown out that possibility days ago. There was, she saw, no point in discussing her worries here. The facts were too complicated to explain easily; there were too many blurred areas of uncertainty, guesswork, surmise. They sat and ate for a while without speaking, other people's conversations swooping around them.

'So what's your new schedule got in store for the rest of the week?' Sandra said at last. 'Tell me everything.'

It was a relief to move away from Terry and Marie spoke with a new brightness. 'Well, you know I'm on the management team now. We're having a meeting tomorrow at half six. I'm just presenting the monthly figures from our department. Nothing that exciting.'

'You never know,' said Sandra, 'I suppose we'll have to stop meeting like this, now.'

Marie stared at her, confused. 'How come?'

'Hanging out with the staff? It's just not done, Marie. Might make you biased.'

There was a long, uncomfortable pause in which Marie grasped the truth of what Sandra had said: she wasn't one of the girls any more, and acting as if she was might make her look unprofessional. Then Sandra spoke again: 'Well, suppose we'd better get the bill and head back.'

'Sure,' said Marie, and they did.

During the brief walk back to work, neither woman spoke. Marie felt a nameless chill. She'd always prized closeness and companionship, but it felt as if they were slipping away from her even as other things arrived: promotion closing a door between her and a long-term work friend . . . and something sinister that she couldn't place blurring communication between her and Terry. Again she remembered the empty desk he'd been sitting at last night and shivered.

16

Terry's day passed impossibly slowly, as his days at work always did now. He worked on copy for a minor clothing catalogue, and Rodge worked on the design at the desk across from his own. The two rarely spoke. They weren't friends at any level, and Terry knew it, but sometimes he tried to lie to himself that they were. It was too bitter to come to terms with his isolation here.

Too much like the past, Terry? Is that it?

Minutes ticked out in the bottom right-hand corner of his computer screen. The window beside him showed deepening grey streets seven floors up, tiny windows well lit and detailed against the gathering evening. Fluorescent lights buzzed. He wouldn't be betraying Marie, Terry told himself, by seeking out the black-haired girl after work. There was something oddly asexual about his fascination with her – a creature from another world who thought in a different way, lived, felt, existed.

At five thirty, Rob and Christian went over to the rickety old table-football machine in the corner, and began their afternoon game. They had a detailed office league table in operation, charting their prowess with the plastic players, and Viv Sacker treated their hobby with a tolerant, indulgent amusement. *Boys will be boys*, his eyes said, as he walked past them. *After all, they're young.* Rodge rose from his computer and hovered round the edges of the group, and tried to get them to play him. Terry didn't: he couldn't see the sense in setting himself up for further rejection. He thought that Rodge's desperation to be accepted by the loud, laddish clique was as pitiful as it was pointless, but of course, he'd never tell him so: there was no point. Rodge only ever listened to people he considered important.

There was nothing to keep him in the office now. In the old days of success and client meetings, he'd stayed regularly till seven or eight but now there was nothing in his workload he couldn't complete by half five. Switching off his computer, he rose from his seat, hearing the noise from the table-football, the voices that rebounded and rang out as harshly as the ball did. 'Oh you bastard!' Rob was howling. 'That's it! I'm going to thrash you now.'

Terry put on his coat. 'Well, see you tomorrow,' he said, to nobody in particular. 'Have a good night.' But nobody seemed to hear him, and he left the office unobserved.

He was the only person in the mirrored lift that took him down to the ground floor, where he smiled briefly at the pallid teenager on Reception before stepping out into the cold. Already it was dark, and streetlights burned orange and yellow on the crowded evening. People drank *cappuccino* and *latte* in coffee shops, and stared out at the ebb and flow of passing strangers with flat, incurious eyes. And Terry walked alone, turning towards the noise and alien vivacity of Soho's heart, full of a sense of *déjà vu* that hit him hard.

Remember those slow days in the classroom, Terry? How lonely you felt. And there was never any comfort going home. No wonder you started going for those walks when the hometime bell rang. A few months before Katie died. Remember those country lanes? The sharp smells, the green smells. The dream you kept having then. You thought about it while you were walking, Terry. What you could do to change things – what you wanted more than anything else . . .

Through a tangled forest of neon, music and shrieking

laughter, Terry walked in the bright light of a remembered summer afternoon, trying to forget the recurring dream he'd had back then. It seemed no time at all before he was seeing the distant red scrawl that spelt out Delilah's on the night, and walking towards it as if hypnotised, slowly approaching a deeper darkness that he wanted far too badly.

17

The narrow stairs gave way to the too-opulent reception area. The heavy red-velvet curtains stirred in a breeze that Terry couldn't feel.

'Good evening, sir,' said the little lizard-like man in neat black and white, taking his jacket across the desk. 'Have a nice evening.'

'I will,' said Terry, and it didn't sound like the same voice that had called an unheard goodbye to an indifferent office, and he didn't feel like the same man who'd sat ignored in the meeting that morning, wondering how his life had gone so wrong. Because this was a place of dreams, and in a place of dreams you could be anyone you wanted.

Had he felt like this the last time he'd come here? He couldn't quite remember . . .

Through the curtains, the thin rosy lights intensified his sense of unreality. The disco globe spun points of light across the men and girls who talked and drank champagne at the tables and the blonde girl who writhed snakelike on the dance-floor, oiled and gleaming in a white string bikini, anonymous as a fantasy. Tonight, the club seemed more than ever like another world, and he saw its depth and its details with a new immediacy as he wondered when the black-haired girl would arrive.

'What would you like, sir?' asked the barman, approaching.

'I'll have a Jack Daniel's,' he said, 'on the rocks.' He paid and sipped and watched and waited, before suddenly realising that he was waiting for nothing. The girl who'd haunted his mind all weekend was already there.

He hadn't seen her because she was sitting at the back of the room, talking closely with a middle-aged man in a dark business suit. Champagne rested in an ice-bucket in the centre of the table. As Terry watched, a young waiter stopped to top up their glasses, and her face drew closer to the middle-aged man's. She tilted her head back and laughed.

It was, he thought, like looking at an unattainable freedom across the bar – he had the feeling that this infatuation had nothing to do with his relationship with Marie. He didn't want to sleep with this girl, just to know her, her liberty and lawlessness, the way she didn't seem to care about anything in the world. He watched her and raised his glass to his lips, tasting the thrill of corruption, fearing and relishing it, wanting more.

When he saw her rise from the table, he was instantly alert. She passed him, heading towards the door marked Ladies. He put a hand on her arm, and spoke quickly. 'I want to talk to you.'

She looked at him, apparently without surprise. 'I'm sitting with someone now. What do you want?'

Her voice was unusual, although he didn't know exactly why – it was clear, low, accentless, pleasant, melodious. Perhaps the strangeness lay in the lazy assurance of her delivery, the way she picked her words like flowers for a mixed bouquet. Up close, he noticed that she was older than he'd thought, perhaps twenty-five. 'Just to talk to you,' he said. 'I had to ask.'

Her white forehead creased. 'Why?'

'Because . . .' He couldn't think what to say. 'I saw you here last week.'

'I saw a lot of people here last week.' She laughed; the sound was both childish and dark, cruel in a way he found hard to define. 'It's what I do.'

'You must remember. You smiled.'

'On the stairs. Of course.' Her eyebrows raised a little. 'Did it mean anything?'

'I think it did.' He felt emboldened because she remembered, because perhaps she'd thought of him, too. 'Stay with me a while.'

'I can't. I told you, I'm sitting with someone. I've got to go.'

'Will you be in tomorrow night?'

'I expect so.'

'I'm Terry,' he said quickly. 'What's your name?'

'Rosina.' But she spoke the name over her shoulder, moving through the gathering crush round the bar, through the door marked Ladies. He stood looking after her for a few seconds, then decided to leave. He sensed that this evening had reached its natural zenith, and he didn't want to stay to watch its beauty and mystery fade back into fear.

He set down his glass on the bar and walked out. Through the red velvet curtains, he paid his cloakroom fee to the lizard-like man, who handed him his coat and wished him a good evening. Terry put it on and buttoned it before he went up the stairs and out into the night. As he walked towards the tube station through the cold neon darkness, a clock ticked slowly in his head. His secret half-recognised desires had a name after all, he thought, because she was called Rosina, and he was going to see her tomorrow.

18

Rosina stayed in the toilet cubicle for a few minutes after she'd finished, listening to the furtive murmur of voices in the next cubicle, which meant that someone was buying coke. It was a sound you got used to when you worked here for any length of time. A smile touched the corners of her lips as she heard Christine's voice in her mind: *I'm scared of drugs. I don't want to take that, Rosina.*

She unbolted the cubicle door and stepped out. Vicki and a girl called Roxanne were spraying on perfume. They looked round as she came over and started to wash her hands. 'Hey,' said Vicki, 'saw you talking to that bloke just now.'

'What bloke?'

'You know,' said Vicki, curious, slightly impatient. 'The gorgeous one.'

Rosina's shoulders rose and fell, and she said nothing.

'*Rosina*,' said Vicki. 'What did he say to you?'

'He asked me what my name was,' Rosina said offhandedly. 'Asked me if I'd be here tomorrow night.'

'Is he coming in to see you?' asked Roxanne.

'I don't know. Maybe.' Behind them, the cubicle door opened at last. Two dancers hurried out and past them. Rosina registered their faces in the mirrors, her own betraying nothing. *You always notice things, Rosina*, murmured Christine, *I wish I was like you*, and she took a red lipstick out of her bag, and reapplied it in silence.

'You're sitting with that suity bloke, aren't you?' asked Vicki.

'Yeah.'

'You don't seem in much of a hurry.'

'Why hurry? He's not going anywhere.' Rosina put away her lipstick, saw Vicki and Roxanne watching her with eyes that didn't quite know what to make of her. 'He's very boring. They usually are.'

'Except the gorgeous bloke,' said Vicki, gathering her things together.'

'Maybe,' said Rosina.

As the door swung shut behind Vicki and Roxanne, Rosina met her own eyes in the mirror, and thought about the blond man called Terry she'd just spoken to. Perhaps he *wasn't* boring, she thought, but it wasn't really his pale good looks that attracted her. Something about him called out to her and reminded her of things that now lay in the past – tentative, longing, ripe for corruption as a silly little girl named Christine had been, long ago.

I'm scared, said Christine plaintively, and Rosina smiled her complicated little smile as she picked up her bag, walked out of the toilets, and returned to the table and the man in the suit.

19

For Marie, there was no way of ignoring the silences that fell over dinner that night. Even though Terry didn't seem to notice them, to her they were glaring.

'When are you going to tell me what's the matter, Terry?'

He looked up from his plate – a defensive expression flickered across his face. 'Nothing's the matter. Really. I've just had a hard day at work. That's all.'

'You've been working hard lately, haven't you?'

He nodded and showed no sign of saying any more. Suddenly, she was gripped by desperation, a need to prove her unidentified suspicions either justified or groundless. 'What are you working on?'

'A big new account we've just won.' She watched him closely, and was about to say something else when he added, 'Homebase. You know, the DIY place.'

Had he paused a split-second too long? Had he told her the first name that came into his head? She castigated herself for ridiculous paranoia, but the suspicion refused to go away. 'And that's what you've been working on in the study?'

'Of course.' He sat and looked at her with confused, wounded eyes. 'What did you think I've been working on?'

'Well, how should I know?' Suddenly, she felt wrong-footed. It was too easy to believe that he'd just tidied away his work before she'd entered the study last night, that he was coping with a mixture of bereavement and a stressful job: in her own mind, she'd built it up into something close to psychosis. 'Do you have to do any more tonight?'

'No. I'm going to have to stay seriously late tomorrow night, though. God knows when I'll be getting back.'

'Don't worry about it. I've got a late meeting myself.' She rose from the table and dished up another helping of roast potatoes. 'I remember you used to work all hours, in the old days. It's a good sign, if you're getting back to that again.'

'*The old days*,' he said, and she felt oddly sorry for him, knowing perfectly well what he was thinking. He'd never been more successful in his career than he'd been then – he'd never earned more, either. She remembered him coming home after an awards ceremony one night, with a statuette under one arm and a bottle of champagne under the other. How unthinkable it would have seemed then that, seven years on, she'd be the major breadwinner in the household. 'Yeah. Maybe it'll all start happening for me again, now.'

'I hope so.' For Marie, seeing through his eyes and feeling with his nerves was poignant. She spoke again: 'Go and put the telly on, why don't you? I'll be out as soon as I've finished washing up.'

He smiled slightly, got up and walked out. Marie scraped the plates clean and stacked the washing-up in the sink. She was, she supposed, old-fashioned about doing all the housework herself; she had always taken a small domestic pleasure in the cosy rituals of a fifties housewife. But now as she washed and wiped, she felt anything but comfortable and contented. She didn't know what to believe. Not tonight.

What was the man in the living-room thinking about? The award he'd won years ago? A heavy workload for a client named Homebase? A dead father he'd never been close to? Or the son he'd never had?

Or was it something else, which he kept shut away in his study and had never told her about in the years of their marriage?

She didn't know. But as she finished the washing-up, Marie found herself thinking that maybe she'd explore that study at some point in the not-so-distant future. For her peace of mind if nothing else.

20

Once it had been unusual for Terry to take a long time getting to sleep. Recently, it had become the norm. In the talcum-scented darkness, he lay awake beside Marie, trying not to wake her too. More than anything he wanted to go back down to the study, but he knew he couldn't risk it. He could see her getting suspicious about his activities in there; he didn't want her to come down unexpectedly, and ask him questions he couldn't answer.

What's the matter, Terry?

As a child, he'd wanted someone to ask him that. Someone to listen, and sympathise, and reassure. A big fat comfortable woman who smelt of Parma violets, whose frequent smiles always reached her eyes. Other children had imaginary friends. In his loneliness and bewilderment, he'd created for himself an imaginary mother. He remembered sleepless nights crowded with asexual, too-vivid fantasies – an anonymous ideal of motherhood tucking him into bed, a vast maternal presence, who loved him more than anyone in the world. He had been adopted, he imagined, and one day his real mother would collect him from the vicarage where he'd never belonged, and she'd have nothing in common with Paul or Julia Fielding, and she'd look at little Katie and feel nothing.

By his eighth birthday, the fantasies had come to an abrupt and painful end. Of course Julia Fielding was his real mother: you only had to look at her to know that – the porcelain skin, the iced-water eyes, the hair so blonde it was almost white. She looked like an older female mirror-image of her son, and the physical resemblance distressed him. He was watched by his own face, and saw that it held nothing but indifference.

She'd been a cold woman, thin and restless, a hundred million miles away from the mother of his dreams; always cleaning or polishing or writing a letter or organising a church fair, always brushing him away with an irritable gesture and a curt, dismissive word. *Run along. Can't you see I'm busy?* She hardly ever used his name, even when it seemed impossible for her not to. *Happy birthday. Merry Christmas. Good night.* If it hadn't been for Katie, he'd have thought her incapable of loving a child, would have grown up thinking it was just the way she was, that she preferred adult company and her own businesslike concerns to the soothing togetherness of motherhood, that she simply wasn't maternal, and it wasn't his fault.

But you were denied that, Terry. God or the Fates or whatever denied you even that, when little Katie came along . . .

How different his mother had been with Katie. Ever since Terry could remember, he'd hated seeing the two of them together, the proof that cold, unreachable Julia Fielding was as capable of love as the woman in his early dreams. With Katie, she smiled and cosseted and worried and played. *Hello, Katie, sweetheart. Look, you've got a leaf caught in your hair.* It felt like watching some dreaded creature become approachable from a distance – a lioness kittenish with her cubs, a she-bear protective of her clumsy, defenceless offspring – knowing it would become terrible all over again if you made the mistake of coming too close. Across the kitchen, across the garden, little Terry watched his mother become kind.

It should have reassured him, he supposed, to know that she was human, but it made his fears worse. She could love happy little golden-haired Katie, but she couldn't love him. Maybe nobody would ever be able to love him. Maybe there was something about him that simply wasn't lovable . . .

And fear fed off itself to make him timid and reserved, which created a barrier between himself and his peers, and he was as lonely and secretly despairing at school as he'd always been at home. He couldn't join in the casual camaraderie of the other boys. Deep inside, he was afraid they'd reject him as his mother had, if he showed them too much of himself.

School and home, home and school. An endless nightmare circle ringed around by indifferent eyes . . .

What's the matter, Terry?

. . . before he'd begun to get angry . . .

He lay in the darkness beside his sleeping wife, feeling then and now merge inexorably into one. He thought of the club after work tomorrow evening, and Rosina, and something else that came before either of them. Suddenly, he needed it more than anything, his secret of secrets, beyond even the hidden things in the study, the one tangible thing he'd been able to salvage from his solitary past.

Tomorrow lunchtime, Terry, the little voice murmured. *Go and see it tomorrow lunchtime.* Something in the voice calmed him. Gradually memories blurred round the edges like smoke, and wove around faces and details from his present life. The night closed in over him. He slept.

21

He kept wanting to talk to Rodge about the way things really were in the office. Whether Rodge was a friend or not, he was almost as isolated as Terry was, and their shared loneliness made them, in some way, the same. It was ridiculous, Terry thought, that they couldn't discuss the things that mattered even when they were alone together, that some unspoken protocol of stubbornness and independence locked them away in separate hells.

'What do you think of Rob and Christian?' Terry asked.

It was half past ten in the morning, and they were sitting together in one of the bleak, anonymous little meeting rooms on the seventh floor. They'd been coming up with one-off concepts for a pizza restaurant, to run in the south London press. Rodge laid his sketch-pad to one side and looked at Terry closely. 'How d'you mean?'

Like a conspirator, he tried to arrange the question in a way that would cast no suspicion on him, that could let him say he'd asked out of idle curiosity only. 'Just – what do you think of them? Do you like them?'

'Of course I like them. What's not to like? They're great lads. A good laugh.' Rodge spoke carelessly and expansively. Only his eyes gave him away. 'You should get to know them, Terry. No need to be scared of them just because they're young.'

He used the word as assiduously, as religiously as Sacker did, but it didn't work for him at all – Terry saw the anxious lines drawn round the mouth, the receding hairline that the ponytail did nothing to hide. 'None of us is getting any younger,' he said, unable to stop himself. 'Even Viv.'

'Yeah. But Viv'll still be hanging on in there when he's sixty. He's a hell of a talent. A great guy.'

'You like Viv?'

'Of course,' said Rodge, and looked back at Terry – ostentatiously devout, insinuating. 'Don't you?'

It was sad, infuriating and lonely to be in the presence of both terror and treachery. Terry didn't know whether to sympathise with Rodge or hate him. 'Of course I do.'

Terry's eyes strayed out of the window. It was raining hard. Small colourful umbrellas moved seven floors down, and distant traffic noise provided the only sound. 'Well,' said Rodge eventually, 'suppose we'd better get on with the brief.'

At half past twelve, they had a break for lunch, and Terry left the office alone. Out of the main reception area, he put up his own umbrella against the rain, and turned towards the impersonal crowds of Oxford Street. He needed his secret too badly this afternoon – like he needed the black-haired girl called Rosina after work.

Through the lunchtime chaos, Terry walked. The wet streets were charcoal-grey, crowded with brightly lit shop windows and a drifting smell like bonfires. 'Roast chestnuts,' an old man was calling listlessly. 'Get your roast chestnuts here.' And Terry pressed deeper into his heavy coat and hurried past, the cold stinging his nose and cheeks as the familiar lights of NatWest came into view, and he crossed the road to meet them.

Inside NatWest, there was no queue for the cashpoint. He approached it and inserted the card Marie didn't know about.

He pressed in his PIN number, then Balance Enquiry. Small green letters flashed endlessly on the screen. PLEASE WAIT, they said, PLEASE WAIT, and between each flash, Terry saw the big, jovial, popular vicar who'd deferred to Julia Fielding like a clumsily adoring dog, who'd fussed over little Katie because Julia did, who'd followed her lead in ignoring Terry as he had in everything else.

He'd left his only son something, at least . . .

PLEASE WAIT, the letters said, and then a row of small numbers was smiling out at Terry from the glass, a five-figure sum that was the only thing in the world he could truly call his own.

22

For long, slow seconds, he stood and looked at it. It seemed to hold him hypnotised. In that time, it was the only thing that existed for him, the solid proof of his father's inheritance, something to have and to hold.

Why hadn't he told Marie as soon as he'd found out about it? The truth he didn't want to admit to himself. He didn't know.

All he knew was that, at one minute he'd been holding back the news over a quiet dinner in the kitchen, preparing to break the silence of bereavement with good news. At the next, he thought he'd left it too late, it would sound strange if he told her now. And an hour later, it had begun to harden into a *bona fide* secret, weighing in his mind to terrify and thrill him simultaneously. Lying in bed beside her that night, it seemed impossible that he could ever have contemplated telling her.

Stupid, he told himself savagely. *Insane. She's your wife, you're supposed to share things like this.* But the voice in his mind lacked persuasive power. The numbers on the screen had become more than the money he and Marie used to pay the mortgage, to buy the groceries, to make a down-payment on a new three-piece suite. They had become a kind of talisman.

Was that irrational? Was he slipping again?

He didn't know that, either. All he knew was that his inheritance had changed into something far beyond the sum of its parts. Slowly, he became aware of the noise and clamour around him – two office girls giggling at the paying-in machine, the queue at the enquiries desk, the throat being cleared immediately behind him, telling him someone was tired of waiting for their turn. He got his card back, replaced it in his wallet and walked out into the grey afternoon. The rain had given way to a monotonous drizzle, and he bought sandwiches at Pret A Manger before returning to Soho Square.

The rest of the day passed predictably, interminably. He and Rodge came up with a few more concepts and returned to the office, agreeing to present their ideas to the account handler in charge of the campaign first thing tomorrow morning. Terry worked on some leaflet copy that was due for the end of the day. By four thirty, he'd finished it and e-mailed it through. He sat back in his seat and gazed out of the window by his desk, which faced on to Tottenham Court Road. Forty-storey Centre Point towered above the deepening winter dusk, and intermittent umbrellas still moved far below – an infinity of tiny windows looked back at him like colour photographs mounted on dark-grey card. He considered how the people in those windows would perceive him, an interchangeable and faceless wage-slave, sitting at a computer in a nameless office, and knew his colleagues and his boss saw him in exactly the same way. Only the red neon sign in his mind marked him out, he thought, along with his secret inheritance, and the things he'd tried his hardest not to think of for twenty-seven years.

Little Katie lying dead in the orchard with a skipping-rope beside her. The headlines that screamed of her murder . . .

Minutes slipped past. The noise from the table-football rang out as Rob and Christian began their evening game, and Rodge hurried to join them. Someone came round with the new phone-lists. Nobody said goodbye to Terry as he left. The lift faded into Reception, which faded into the night where life began – the crowded, well-lit streets under a black sky marbled with clouds, the distant promise of a black-haired girl called Rosina.

23

'And as you all know, we've got a new member of the management team. I expect you're all aware of Marie Fielding.'

Seated at the long, narrow boardroom table between the head of Sales and the head of Finance, Marie smiled round at everyone – a natural smile was rarely an effort for her but it was now. The fourth-floor windows showed nothing but solid black, and the light was stark and pitiless; she suddenly felt out of her depth. Aside from the hard-looking head of Sales, the management team consisted of men and, from the perfunctory smiles that reflected back at her, they didn't seem anywhere near as friendly as the girls in Credit Control.

'If you've had time to get *au fait* with the target figures, Marie,' said the managing director, 'maybe you can start this meeting off with a run-down.'

'Sure,' said Marie, and stood up. She'd always been a confident presenter, and was relieved to find that at least that hadn't changed. She'd prepared photostats of the target figures to hand round the table and, as she did so, the nervousness left her. This wasn't such a big deal, she realised; compared to her worries about Terry, it was a stroll in the country. 'So I think that's pretty much all,' she concluded. 'Unless anyone has any questions?'

Nobody did. She sat down, and was smiled at with rather more warmth. The meeting moved on. The head of Sales spoke of her team's recent achievements, before the head of Marketing took over to say much the same thing. After that, it was the turn of the head of Finance. He was a depressed-looking elderly man, with perhaps the most boring voice Marie had ever heard, and as the minutes dragged past, she found herself praying for him to finish.

The only problem was, he showed no sign of doing any such thing. Every point he made seemed to demand another ten to back it up, and he even expanded on those. Convinced she must have been listening to him for a good half-hour, Marie fought back the urge to check her watch. She glanced across the table, and met the eyes of Robert Hall, head of Strategy.

She hadn't really noticed him when she'd smiled round at the beginning of the meeting – he'd seemed interchangeable with the other besuited, fortysomething men dotted round the table. But as she accidentally made eye-contact, he gave her the warmest and most genuine smile she'd seen all evening, followed by a tiny expression of indescribable eloquence – eyebrows raised by a fraction of a centimetre, the eyes themselves turning up slightly. It summed up everything she was feeling herself. *I'm rapidly losing the will to live*, that expression said. *Surely he can't go on much longer . . .*

For a moment, Marie was convinced she was going to burst out laughing. The droning voice flowed on around her, and she watched her hands intently. She couldn't bring herself to look back at Robert until the head of Finance finally stopped talking and sat down. Then she glanced at him, and he glanced at her, and both smiled slightly.

The managing director's summing-up was mercifully concise, and everyone started getting their papers together. 'Same time next week, everyone,' he said from the head of the table. 'Have a good evening.'

Out of the boardroom, Marie stopped off to touch up her makeup in the ladies'. When she came out, Robert was waiting by the lifts. He turned as she approached. 'So, what did you make of your first meeting?'

If it hadn't been for that small wonderful pantomime of boredom, she'd have answered formally and predictably – he looked so much like the archetypal stuffed-shirt, a tall smartly suited man of perhaps forty-two, with a pleasant, unexceptional face and greying dark hair worn short and neat. But as it was, she detected warmth and humour in the dark eyes, which gave her the confidence to be herself. 'Well, it could have been worse. It could have gone on till midnight.'

'Now you know why they call it a *board* room.' The lift arrived. They got in, he pressed the button for the ground floor. 'But seriously, how are you taking to management? If it's not too soon to ask.'

'It probably is. In a week's time I think I'll know one way or the other,' she said. 'I'm used to just being one of the team.'

'It gets easier.' The lift stopped on the ground floor, and they walked through Reception together. 'Well, see you tomorrow, Marie,' he said, as they stepped out into the chilly darkness and their paths diverged.

'See you. Have a good night.'

Marie checked her watch under a streetlight, and was amazed to see that it was only a quarter to eight. She burrowed deeper into her coat and headed for the tube station. As the escalator took her down, she found herself thinking of Robert with something like affection. He seemed a nice man, she thought.

Then she was boarding the tube, heading for home, and Terry.

24

Rosina had known he'd be in to see her that night, that he'd be there early, and she'd come in to wait for him. She was the first hostess in the club. She stood alone by the bar, wearing black as she always did, waiting for the sharp bell from Reception that told the club a customer was coming.

When it rang, she knew it would be Terry, and it was.

He was even more handsome than she remembered, and,

although it wasn't precisely that which drew her to him, she was grudgingly impressed by his beauty – a pure, cold beauty that made her think of statues in a remembered Chelsea garden. She watched him moving towards her through the club's near-emptiness, heard quiet music drifting through the air like smoke.

'Hello,' she said, as he approached.

Was he nervous? She couldn't tell. He was out of place here, but then she supposed she was herself, and it had never made her feel ill at ease. He stood as still as she did, watching her. 'Were you waiting for me?'

'Of course,' she said. 'I knew you'd come.'

'How did you know when?'

'I just did,' she said. 'You have to buy me a drink, if you want to talk. It's the rules. They watch us.'

'All right.' He sounded mesmerised, which delighted her – the proof of how she drew him. 'What'll you have?'

'Champagne, of course. It's all we can have.' She lowered her voice. 'If you want to talk in private, we should go down to a table. But you have to buy a bottle down there.'

'Then I will,' he said. 'Let's go.'

Across the club, she raised a hand to the old waiter, Karl, whose stint on Reception had ended now that a more suitable candidate had come along, and watched him hurry over. Kark escorted them through the drifting disco lights and the music that was gradually getting louder to a table at the back of the club. 'Here you are, sir,' he said to Terry. 'Be sure to choose something nice for the lady.'

'What'll you order?' she asked.

'I don't know. Does it matter what I choose in here?'

'Not really. Just have what you like.' She reached over the menu he was holding, stroked across the second or third name on the list. 'Maybe that one. It doesn't matter.' And he nodded, and she looked at him looking at her, fixing her attention on his eyes, committing them to memory.

The club was getting busier, filling up with a steady trickle of the loud City boys she disliked and the middle-aged men in dark business suits who reminded her of too much. They came through the heavy red-velvet curtains in twos and threes and fours as Karl returned to Terry. 'Have you chosen for the lady yet, sir?'

'Yeah. We'll have the Lanson.'

'Very good, sir. I shall bring it straight to your table.'

He left. She watched Terry glancing round the club – at the couples now coming down to sit at the tables, the oiled girls writhing on the dance-floor, the drifting points of light from the disco globe – and thought she knew exactly what he was thinking. The darkness in here could draw you. She knew it. It had drawn her.

'Why do you work here?' he asked at last.

'You ask too many questions.' She smiled inside at his innocence and his presumption, the way he seemed to expect her to hand over her soul. If only he knew the truth. 'Do you know that?'

'I'm curious,' he said slowly.

'Why?'

'Because you look like you belong here.'

This time, she couldn't quite stop the smile in her mind from reaching her mouth. 'Should I be flattered?'

'I don't know.' In the corner of her eye, a black girl in a leopardskin bikini writhed against a metal pole. 'You're very beautiful.'

'So are you,' she said gravely. 'I thought that when I first saw you, you know, on the stairs.'

Seconds passed in eye-contact and ambiguous silence. Karl returned with a bottle of champagne in an ice-bucket. 'Would you care to taste the champagne, sir?' he asked, pouring an inch or so into Terry's glass.

She watched him sip and nod.

'Have a good evening, sir,' said Karl, and walked away.

When Karl was out of earshot, Terry leaned close to her. 'Where are you from?'

'Anywhere you want,' she said, and laughed. 'Where do you want?'

'Here.'

'Why?'

'Because I'm not from here.'

The barely suppressed yearning in his voice was like a caress, and she saw the world around them with a new immediacy: the lights from the disco globe swimming lazily over the table and the veiled sensuality of the slow soul song playing, the beauty of anonymity and the loneliness of the night outside. Something about this evening and this man touched her deep inside with an excitement that was more than sexual: in his eyes she sensed potential that thrilled her. 'I suppose you want to leave with me,' she said at last.

His eyebrows rose slightly. 'Don't you have to stay? I thought you worked here.'

'It's not like that here. You could call us . . . freelancers. We don't get paid just for *being* here. Just tips and . . . private earnings. When we leave.' She smiled a small, secret smile at the club's labyrinthine rules she'd come to know inside out over the past few years; she realised how new he was to all this. 'We can leave with a man whenever we like, as soon as he's bought a bottle of champagne at a table.'

'Would you leave with me?'

'Of course,' she said. 'We can't just walk out together, though. It's too obvious. Management doesn't like it.'

'Well, I'll meet you outside. Nearby.'

To some extent, she found it easy to see through his eyes, feel the rosy side-lamps and the champagne giving him courage. She thought she knew what he was going to say next, but his next words surprised her. 'I do want to leave with you. Not to sleep with you. Just to be alone with you. Just to talk.'

She looked back at him, more than ever intrigued. So he thought he was good, wore his fidelity as ostentatiously as his wedding ring. It didn't matter. In time she'd show him what he really was, and it would be all the more fun for waiting. 'All right,' she said. 'You can.'

25

I'll meet you in five minutes, she'd said. *Wait outside Austin Reed.*

He did.

The rain had stopped, and the crowds had thinned out to occasional passers-by who paid him no attention. He leaned back against dank brickwork and looked into still-luminous shop windows. The serene white mannequins had an eerie look now that neon and darkness reflected off the window-glass. Far away, a police siren howled. He listened to it fade slowly into the city night, and waited.

He thought of Marie at home, remembered that she wouldn't be worrying about his whereabouts, that he'd prepared the ground in the kitchen, last night: *I'm going to have to stay seriously late tomorrow night, though. God knows when I'll be getting back.* It was strange to think he'd prepared an alibi in advance before he'd known how tonight would turn out. A part of him had been standing here, waiting, even then.

No need for guilt, even though it threatened to engulf him at any second. He wasn't really being unfaithful.

He saw her coming towards him. She wore a heavy black coat that covered her completely, and her heels tapped out on the pavement. As she approached, he discovered he still thought of her as unreachable, and knew that part of him always would. Even now that he knew her name and had talked to her, he couldn't help seeing her as a girl from a fantasy, eternally distant and unknown.

Then she was there. They fell into step together.

'Where shall we go?'

'There's a hotel I know in Victoria,' she said. 'We'll have to get a taxi.'

They hailed the next one that passed. Water sprayed from the puddles as it stopped to let them in. She gave quick terse instructions to the cabbie, and they sat side by side, gazing out of separate windows. Terry watched the cheap, cheerful chaos of Piccadilly Circus unfolding beyond them, the bleakness of Trafalgar Square, the floodlit majesty of Whitehall. The sight overwhelmed him, and when her hand touched his, he wanted to take it and squeeze it to make sure she was real.

'Almost there,' she whispered. 'Not long now.'

The hotel was medium-sized and impersonal, as sleazily indifferent as the man behind the reception desk. In the harsh light of the foyer, his black hair shone like patent leather as he greeted them with seen-it-all-before eyes. Terry paid by card, and no further details were asked for.

'Room 225,' the man said, doling out a chunky roomkey. 'Lift's broken. You'll have to take the stairs.'

They walked. Terry wanted to take Rosina's hand, but a recurring image of Marie stopped him. He was intensely attracted to this girl: the asexual nature of his fascination had changed, making physical contact with her both longed-for and dangerous. The silence seemed to last a very long time.

'It's expensive here,' he said eventually.

Her shoulders rose and fell, with a cool, offhand amusement that he was beginning to recognise as characteristic of her. 'It's as cheap as it gets.'

'I suppose it is,' he said uncertainly. 'But I'm not rich.'

'I knew that as soon as I saw you.'

'But you spoke to me. The other girls wouldn't have, if they'd known.'

'I'm not like them,' she said, as they came out on to a wide, empty landing. 'I don't want money. Not from you.'

'What do you want?' He stopped at a door, turned the key.

Her smile was a flicker in the corner of his eye. 'Everything.'

The door swung open. Terry saw a seedy, impersonal room with a wide low bed and a darkened doorway that could only lead to the bathroom. Through the small window, a streetlight burned sodium-yellow, corrupting the moonlight with a sallow edge. Rosina kicked off her shoes and sat down hard on the bed. It squeaked beneath her. 'What do *you* want,' she asked idly, 'if you don't want sex?'

He was jolted by the ease with which she spoke the word. More than ever, he felt her distance from him. 'I don't know. Just to talk.'

'What about?'

'You.'

In the glow from the streetlight, her face was unearthly, dappled with reflected raindrop patterns. 'So ask me something.'

He thought it would be hard to think of a specific question, was surprised to feel one come as easy as breathing. 'Where are you really from?'

She laughed again, this time almost tenderly. 'What kind of question's that?'

'I want to know everything about you,' he said. 'Where?'

'I'm not sure you'd believe me.'

'*Tell* me.'

He watched the curl of her lips in the shadows. 'Chelsea sometimes. Sometimes Cirencester.'

'Why Cirencester?'

'We had a house there. For weekends. And one in the Dordogne. For summer.'

He looked at her, unsure whether or not to believe her. 'So why *this? Now?*'

She sat up so that her feet were on the bed, and hugged her knees close to her chest. It was a childish, impulsive gesture that made her habitual cold grace even more compelling. Her pale blue eyes watched him above the gawky pose with a secret, somehow malicious expression. 'Because I want to. I always do what I want to.'

'Slumming?'

'No,' she said. 'Freedom.'

She bewildered him – he had the dreamlike, thrilling sense of being alone in another world. 'What do your parents do?'

'My mother never did anything much. My father was in construction,' she said. 'Parker Bailey. He was Parker.'

He'd seen the name on the sides of lorries and building-sites, but hadn't known it was worth paying attention to –

hadn't associated it with fearlessness and liberty, with the tantalising nearness of a fantasy come true. 'I've heard of it.'

'Yeah. Everyone has,' she said. 'I don't get money from them, if that's what you're thinking. I don't even speak to them any more. Haven't been in touch with them for years.'

His eyes never let her. 'Why not?'

'Because . . . You ask too many questions.'

Her words, throwaway on the surface, had an undercurrent of finality that he caught. Silence pressed in hard. The nonsensical nature of the evening occurred to him – paying a nightly rate for a sleazy room just to talk, then going home – but while he understood that it might be seen as ridiculous, it didn't *feel* ridiculous. Her words had made hungry where most they satisfied, and she fascinated him even more than she had when she'd been a stranger.

'I should go,' he said, when the silence had lasted long enough to become oppressive. 'I've got to go home.'

And she watched him with pale blue eyes that missed nothing, and she nodded, and she smiled.

26

At five to ten Marie was relieved, despite herself, to hear footsteps heading for the front door, telling her Terry was home. She'd spent too long on her own in the house, with no distractions but the half-formed fears she'd been trying to get rid of all day. Telling herself there wasn't anything to worry about in a voice that grew less certain with each minute of solitude. She went to the door, wanting security, reassurance, normality. '*There* you are, Terry. I was starting to think you'd been kidnapped.'

'Sorry. I told you I was going to be late in tonight.'

He kissed her briefly on the cheek and walked past her into the kitchen. She'd been keeping a chicken casserole warm, and put on her oven gloves to get it out. 'Time we were eating,' she said briskly. 'Hope it hasn't gone cold.'

'It doesn't matter,' he said, absently. 'I don't mind.'

He's had a hard day at work, she told herself. *Of course he seems a bit preoccupied – he must be knackered.* She filled his plate, set it down in front of him. 'So how was your day at work?'

'Fine,' he said quickly. 'It was fine.'

She struggled to maintain her bright affectionate smile. His evasive vagueness irritated her. 'Good,' she said. Then, desperate to draw him into something resembling a real conversation: 'I had my first management meeting today, after work.'

She waited for him to ask her about it, but he didn't. Across the table, his downcast eyes were fixed on his food as he ate. Her mingled unease and irritation returned, lingered, and she spoke too sharply: 'Well, don't you want to know how it went?'

He glanced up at her, startled. 'Of course, Marie. What happened?'

'Boring. The head of Finance has to be the dullest man on the face of this earth. I looked at my watch when I thought it was midnight, and it was only half seven.' It was painful to see her attempt at humour met with a half-hearted smile and eyes that were somewhere else – out of the blue, she thought of Robert. 'There's a work do after hours tomorrow,' she said. 'I think I'll stay till eleven or so.'

'Whatever you like.'

Inexplicably, he sounded hurt and sullen. She wanted to ask why, but knew that she wouldn't get an honest answer.

After they'd finished eating and she'd washed up, they spent a quiet, and to her uneasy, hour watching television in the living room, and went to bed at half eleven. She fell asleep while he was brushing his teeth, tiredness and uncertainty turning into something like an anaesthetic, carrying her away into dreams of *film-noir* monochrome, billowing curtains in the night, mysterious shadowed ledges that led to hundred-foot drops.

She was falling through empty air when she woke with a sharp little cry in her throat, and her eyes snapped open. She turned in the bed to face her sleeping husband and see if she'd disturbed him. But there was no sleeping husband. Terry wasn't there.

It was like an action replay of that night last week, only worse. Now she knew exactly where he was. In the study. Alone with the secrets he'd never shared with her – the things he'd never let her understand.

He'll come back to bed soon, she told herself fiercely. *Just forget about it, go back to sleep.* But she knew that was impossible. She wanted and needed to know what Terry was doing, and before she'd made any conscious decision to go downstairs and find out, she was getting out of bed, padding along the landing, down the moonlit stairs, into the hallway. She saw the thin rectangle of light round the closed study door, at first with gnawing fear, then with a kind of defiance.

I've got a right to know, she thought starkly. *I'm his wife, for Christ's sake.* She turned the handle, and the door swung open.

An image imprinted itself behind her eyes: Terry sitting at the desk with his back to her, apparently reading a large book. She felt a moment's relief at the normality of the scene before he whirled round. There was nothing normal about the look in his eyes. They held nothing but screaming terror, and his arm flew to conceal the book.

Instantly, her heart was racing, and she was amazed by the calm in her voice. 'Terry, what are you doing?'

He didn't answer. The terrified expression had been replaced by something else – something wary and hunted that concealed itself behind an unconvincing smile. 'What's the matter?'

'It's almost four o'clock in the morning, Terry,' she heard herself say. 'You should be getting some sleep.'

'I know. I'll be up in a minute, Marie. Just go back to bed.'

There didn't seem to be anything else to say. She went back

upstairs, slid between sheets that had grown chilly. In the darkness, she lay unmoving, staring at the ceiling with her heartbeat pounding in her ears. When she heard his footsteps on the stairs, she turned over and pretended to be asleep, but it was no good. Even when Terry was lying beside her and snoring gently, she didn't get a wink of sleep before the world started to lighten, and the alarm went off by the bed.

27

Rosina sat in the back of the cab looking out into the darkness, seeing her reflection drawn on it like a sketch in white crayon. Going back to the black-walled room that always smelt of Escape, she found images from the past running through her mind. The few words that she'd spoken to Terry had dredged up memories from the bottom of her consciousness – things she tried not to think of, these days – and they wouldn't go away.

You're so lucky, Rosina, said silly overawed Christine. *I wish I could have parents like yours . . .*

She didn't like to admit she could still be hurt by the memory now that she was twenty-three years old, but she could, and was. A mother and father she'd never really known, two glamorous strangers in a silver frame. Beautiful, preoccupied Annabel Parker, who drifted in and out of rooms with a cat's languid self-absorbed indifference, and a casual word that meant nothing. 'Hello, dear. How was your day at school?' she asked, and never really listened to the answer. Heavy-set pompous Leo, so similar to some of the men at the club, forever busy at the office and only seen rarely. His condescending good-fellowship rang out with the arrogance of a thousand board meetings. 'Evening, girls,' he said. 'What on earth have you done to your hair, Rosina?' In a beautiful house in Chelsea, the occasional unsettling presence of two strangers –

I'd give anything for parents like yours, Rosina.

Don't be stupid, Chris. I hate them. They never pay me any attention.

Rosina sat and looked out and remembered the veiled, simmering tensions in her parents' marriage and how she'd hated being alone with them, the isolation of not even being able to tell her best friend. Knowing that she simply wouldn't understand. *You don't know how lucky you are, Rosina*, wept Christine. *You've got everything. Everything.* And she blinked away the memory savagely, but it returned as immediately as the threat of tears.

A three-storey townhouse in an elegant tree-lined street. From the outside, you wouldn't have known it had a garden; from the inside, you wouldn't have known you were in London. French windows faced on to a crowded, colourful paradise of mimosa, rhododendrons and ivy-clad walls. It had been beautiful, Rosina remembered. As the taxi cruised through the empty urban small hours, it occurred to her that she could never tell Terry how deeply she felt her banishment from that paradise. Or why.

Then the streets were becoming familiar, and she was going home.

28

Terry kept thinking of Rosina's laughter. Its cadences seemed to hold the secret of her allure and her magnetism – not carelessness, although the casual listener might have mistaken it for carelessness, but a kind of offhand precision he'd never encountered before, which seemed peculiar to her. It was the defining note of everything she did: the slow curl of her lips when she smiled, the smooth cold hand brushing his own in the back of the taxi, the air of ambiguous amusement she seemed to carry with her everywhere. The amorality of that laughter echoed in his mind, and it seemed that he'd heard it in his dreams before he'd ever met her.

Think about her, then, Terry. Anything but Marie. She really suspects now, you know. How much did she see last night in the study?

'Well,' said Gavin the account handler, approaching him and Rodge. 'Got some great ideas to show me, I hope?'

'Of course.' Rodge gathered up his sketch-pad, the final concepts he'd decided on with Terry that morning. 'We can go to one of the meeting rooms on the seventh. You're going to love these.'

Terry was never sure whether to envy or pity Rodge's brash confidence. It was the product of failure and desperation, just like his own increasing reticence, but the same stimulus had sent the two men in different directions. Watching him spread out the ideas on the meeting-room table, you wouldn't have thought Rodge had a care in the world. 'We tried to stay away from anything too sophisticated,' Rodge was saying. 'It would have been all wrong for the target audience. So, as you see, we've come up with . . .'

Puns and clichés. Uninspired and uninspiring. They'd been the best he and Rodge had been able to muster, but Terry cringed from the sight of them just the same – sneering out from the small round table, in the same little room where Rob and Christian came up with award-winning concepts. They'd laugh at these ideas, he thought starkly. I'd have laughed at them, ten years ago. 'This one's our personal favourite,' said Rodge. ' "Get a slice of the action." With a visual of a slice of pizza. Could be seriously eye-catching.'

Did Rodge know how tired the headlines were? Of course he must. Like Terry, Rodge had been good once. The loud, confident salesman's voice meant nothing when you saw the flicker of the eyes. Gavin's held a mixture of disappointment and stoicism that Terry found horribly easy to interpret. *I knew they'd come up with something like this*, those eyes said, *the ageing hippie and the pretty-boy, the boring, talentless old farts. It's high time Viv got rid of them both.* 'Yeah,' Gavin said dismissively. 'They're all right. Could you get them worked up by the end of the day, Rodge? I'd like to present them to the client tomorrow.'

Back in the office, Sacker called an impromptu meeting in his inner sanctum – there weren't enough chairs to go round so only Rob and Christian sat down. The rest lounged against walls and in the open doorway, waiting for Sacker to speak. 'I've just got our department's tickets to the awards do this Friday,' he said expansively, regretfully. 'Not quite as many as I'd been hoping for, alas. I'm afraid, this time round, it's just Rob, Christian, Alex and Lucy. Only the nominees.'

Hired tuxedos and free champagne, camaraderie round the agency table and shrieked congratulations when the result was read from the podium. Terry wished he couldn't see it so clearly in his memory. 'Hopefully, next time round, there'll be room for a few more of you,' Sacker continued, 'but I thought I'd better make it *absolutely* clear that I'm not deliberately leaving anyone out.'

Terry stood and smiled with the others, knowing he'd never get invited to another awards ceremony as long as he lived. The golden days were over, leaving nothing but Marie's increasing suspicion; the long, solitary hours of terror in the study when he reminded himself of what he had to guard against now that things were going wrong. It all seemed part of this meeting, somehow, a single, coherent whole – the wary eyes in the small hours of the morning, the constant near-terror of discovery—

But there *were* things worth having in his life and, as Sacker's smooth, well-modulated voice rose and fell interminably, he forced himself to remember that. Some aspects of his world and his history were more than pathetic; a row of tiny numbers on a cashpoint screen, a red neon sign in the darkness, Rosina's irresistible laughter lingering in the byways of a dream.

And your sister, Terry. Little Katie.

Lying dead.

29

Marie didn't know why she was surprised that she couldn't get into the party mood that evening. After last night – her husband's look of terror in the study, his hand flying to conceal what she could hardly see – she was more than a little distracted. Not to mention exhausted. Half-formed suspicions gnawed at her mind, murmured behind the loud, squealing music in the Texan-themed bar. She sat at a table by the window and talked to Carol Ellis, head of Sales, wanting more than anything to be somewhere else.

'So, we should be having the Christmas party at Strawberry Moons up West, after all,' Carol was saying. 'We wanted to have it at Mint but they were asking ten grand to book out the downstairs bar, and . . .'

Out of the corner of her eye, Marie saw Sandra, Cheryl and a couple of the other Credit girls leaving in a giggling group and felt a sense of loss like homesickness. She'd been there once, she thought, happy in her marriage, carefree. She saw Robert talking to the managing director by the bar, and suddenly couldn't wait to leave. When a gap presented itself in Carol's strident monologue, she struggled to wedge in words of her own. 'I think I'll go home in a minute, Carol. I don't feel too well.'

'*Already?*' Carol was affronted. 'It's not even nine o'clock yet, Marie.'

'I've got a bit of a headache,' Marie lied. 'I think I'm just in need of an early night, to tell you the truth.' But Carol didn't look remotely sympathetic, and it was a relief to say goodbye and break away.

Outside, it was icy cold, and the thumping beat of the company party followed her for a few steps before it faded into silence. As she headed for the tube station, she was still thinking about Terry and last night. *What was he looking at? What could he have been looking at?*

Throughout their marriage, she'd never snooped through the things he kept in the study – it had always seemed an insult to his privacy. Now, though, the idea didn't seem anywhere near so bad. And it wasn't the distant possibility it had been a few days ago, but something as real and immediate as the prospect of taking out the rubbish – something she had to do.

Next time she was alone in the house she'd look, and she'd find.

She promised herself.

30

In the study, Terry sought out memories of Katie, but when they came to him unbidden, they never failed to unnerve and worry him. He wished the egregious little voice in his mind hadn't reminded him of her like that during the meeting. She stayed with him on the way home as she had all afternoon at work, competing for space with Rosina's laughter, and the club he wanted so badly to go back to that evening.

Couldn't go two nights running: even though he wasn't being unfaithful to Marie, he couldn't afford to let her get suspicious.

Strap-hanging in the stuffy, overcrowded hell of the tube, he looked at nobody and nobody looked at him. His sister smiled behind his eyes. He remembered running back to the house in which they'd been brought up with his heart in his mouth, pounding towards the half-open back door. His mother looking round from peeling potatoes, her habitual chilly irritation snapping into panic as he spoke. 'It's Katie,' he said, 'you've got to come quickly. *I think Katie's dead . . .*'

Then the metallic clash and rattle of the carriages brought him sharply back to the here and now, and the sun-drenched vicarage kitchen seemed a long way away.

By the time he reached Streatham Hill, it was almost seven o'clock and dark – light from newsagents, pubs and street-lamps glowed pallid on the gathering night. Traffic stirred in intermittent waves as he turned down the street where he and Marie lived. He badly needed security and domesticity right now – cooking smells drifted into the hallway, the kitchen table laid for two, lights in the downstairs windows welcoming him home.

But there were no lights on in the downstairs windows.

He reached into his pocket for his key and let himself in. The house was dark and silent. The overhead striplight in the kitchen stuttered on to show nothing but emptiness.

Where the hell was Marie? Try as he might to make the inner voice sharp and matter-of-fact, the words came out with a child's bewilderment. And he could see the child in question far too clearly: an eight-year-old boy who'd come home from school early one afternoon to find nobody in. They'd been picking apples in the orchard, but of course he hadn't known that then. He'd looked for them around the house, full of the greatest fear of his life, long after it had become obvious that they weren't there. They'd always neglected him, but now they'd actually abandoned him – his parents and little Katie.

He knew Marie wouldn't be upstairs, but went to check all the same. There didn't seem anything much else he could do. He returned to the kitchen feeling more afraid than ever. It was ridiculous and it was impossible, but it was also true. She'd *gone.*

Then the front door creaked open, and she was there.

'Hello, Terry,' she said cheerfully. 'Didn't think you'd be home till later. You been in long?'

Almost immediately relief changed to new fear – her bright smile seemed unconsciously to mock his paranoia of a moment ago. 'About five minutes. Where have you *been*?'

Her eyebrows shot up. 'To my work do. I told you about it last night.'

Of course. He could have kicked himself – he'd forgotten all about it. But her voice brought an echo of his mother's, twenty-eight years ago: *There's no need to make such a silly fuss. We were only in the orchard.*

'Well, I *forgot*,' he said now. 'I didn't know where the hell you were. I was *worried*.'

'Well, all's well that ends well. I'm back now.' She walked over to the fridge. 'Suppose I'd better get the dinner on, then. I don't know about you but I'm starving.'

He couldn't think of anything to say. He sat at the kitchen table and watched her back. It wasn't paranoia or imagination, he realised, she really was changing: everything in her eyes and her voice said that she was beginning not to need him. He felt as if he'd awoken from a nightmare to find it was true after all. Across the kitchen, she chopped and peeled in silence. He decided he'd go back to the club after work tomorrow. In the club, with Rosina, fear didn't exist.

31

How he'd hated going to school in the mornings. While he'd been too young then to rationalise the reasons why, looking back he found it was simplicity itself to put a name to them: the way that anxiety had crawled inside him as soon as the tall metal gates came into sight, and he'd felt himself becoming the boy others saw – the timid hanger-on in other people's friendships, the observer of other people's camaraderie, the laugher at other people's jokes. The boy he despised beyond expression. There had to be something beyond the insipid, colourless shell, and part of him had begun to suspect that there was, beginning both to fear and long for his secret potential to fulfil itself. But in the classroom, the half-wonderful, half-awful suspicions ended. They all perceived him as meaningless, powerless. Maybe they were right.

He was starting to feel exactly the same way about the office.

He sat at his desk and worked. It might have been copy for a pizza restaurant or an English comprehension exercise – the buzz of other people's conversation washed over the boy they'd all written off as uninteresting, the boy who always kept quiet and did as he was told. 'Well, I'm not looking forward to the fucking thing,' Rob was complaining loudly. 'I hate getting dressed up like some poncey twat and talking to fucking *clients.* Bunch of boring old bastards, they all are.'

'Come on,' said twenty-five-year-old Alex, fellow nominee for an award – more callous than any of them, not quite as obviously sycophantic as Rodge. 'Bet you'll scrub up lovely in a tux.'

'You know where you can stick your tux,' said Rob, and laughter rolled. Terry listened to the hard lads uproarious at the back of the class before the teacher came in, perceived their unthinking confidence as the badge of membership to some exclusive club. They'd never know how it felt to be afraid. 'I'll give you a clue.'

'Don't worry. I can guess,' said Alex. 'Hey, aren't you supposed to be in the Fanta meeting? Saw Christian heading off to it about ten minutes ago.'

'Shit, yeah,' said Rob. Terry saw him gather some notes together with a total lack of urgency. 'See you later,' he said, and then he was gone.

Terry needed to be somewhere, anywhere else. He rose from his desk abruptly. 'I'm going to make a coffee,' he said to Rodge. 'Want one?'

'Oh, all right.' Rodge didn't look round from his computer screen as he spoke. 'Black. Two sugars.'

Out in the kitchen, Terry filled the kettle and stood waiting for it to boil, trying not to think about anything. The silence was broken by the entrance of two thirtysomething female account handlers he vaguely recognised but didn't know by name. Generally, they stared at him, but today they didn't even register his presence. They came in talking animatedly, in voices so low that they were almost inaudible. People often came into the kitchen to discuss confidential issues away from their boss. The vast open-plan offices made private conversations impossible.

'I don't believe it,' one said. 'We've been seriously busy lately, as well.'

'Well, it's been on the cards for a while,' said the other. 'I blame the management. They waste Christ knows how much on *conference weekends* and that bloody *feng-shui* woman, and then – what do you know? They're up shit creek and have to *let people go.* Bunch of out-of-touch morons.'

Standing on the other side of the kitchen, Terry kept his eyes fixed on the kettle and tried to look as though he wasn't listening while he strained to catch every word. 'You reckon it'll be anyone in our team?' the first account handler said.

'Christ knows. You heard Jim in the meeting just now. We won't know for weeks.' The second account handler sighed, lowered her voice even further. 'Oh, well. At least it's not just us who've got to worry.'

'Wonder when Viv's going to be calling *his* lot in for the news,' muttered the first. 'Jim said the creatives were going to be affected too.'

He couldn't stay in the kitchen any longer. The kettle had boiled seconds ago and, in another minute, his silent presence would be noticed. Terry topped up the brown granules in his and Rodge's mugs with water, added sugar and headed back to the creative department. He set Rodge's coffee beside him and sat down at his desk.

'Cheers,' said Rodge absently, and drank.

Terry was relieved that Rodge was intent on his computer screen and showed no sign of looking round. He didn't need a mirror to see the fear in his eyes, didn't want Rodge to spot it. So this was it, he thought, the dreaded redundancies had come at last. From this moment on, he was living on borrowed time. Beyond the window, he saw the evening closing in, and needed the club and Rosina more than ever.

32

Rosina always came to work ready-dressed in her evening clothes. Vicki and most of the others usually turned up in jeans and trainers and changed in the toilets, but the idea of doing that had never felt quite right to her: it seemed too businesslike and mundane, as if it was a job like any other, and she was doing it solely for the money. And she wasn't doing it just for the money: there was a deeper motivation, and she'd always known it. It had to do with decadence and intricate power games, and the man who was coming to see her this evening. Terry hadn't said he'd be there, but she knew he would. He epitomised the allure of a shadowy world where nobody knew your true identity, where you were free to become anything or anyone you wanted. The expression in his eyes when he looked at her said it all.

You do it, Rosina, silly little Christine had said. *I'm scared* . . .

She could never tell Terry why she wasn't welcome in the beautiful house in Chelsea these days. But now that she had him, she felt the stark fact of her exile less keenly. The night before, in the shadows of a cheap hotel, she'd rediscovered a crucial aspect of that distant time, an echo from the days of the white-and-pinewood bedroom, and holiday snaps from the house in the Dordogne. Absolute adoration, and the power to corrupt . . .

Walking through the streets to work, she remembered silly little Christine more vividly than she had for some time. How she'd grown to despise Christine's fawning infatuation with the girl who had everything. When she'd seen their two faces together in a mirror, she'd felt nothing but contempt for the baby-faced blonde with the scared, overawed look in her eyes, her naked adoration for a girl she'd never be and a world she'd never have. *Love your clothes, Rosina. Love your garden, Rosina. Love your watch, Rosina.* It was all she'd ever really said, apart from the helpless protestations of fear. What a pathetic child she'd been, Rosina remembered. How good it had felt to destroy her.

Inside the club, the toilets were deserted. She flicked her hair back in the mirror, and looked into pale blue eyes that knew too much. Terry would never understand the things that really drove her, she thought, and knew that his ignorance was exactly what made him so attractive to her – the knowledge that he'd be stunned if she told him the truth about herself.

You always have secrets, Rosina, murmured Christine plaintively, and Rosina left the toilets and waited by the bar for Terry's arrival.

33

He entered the club at five to six. It was usually quiet at this time, but not as dead as this. Even the dancers hadn't arrived yet, and apart from the two of them, the shirtsleeved barman was the only person in the place.

'Hello,' she said.

He looked around, in apparent confusion. 'Where is everyone?'

'Who knows? It's like this sometimes. You'll get used to it.' She laughed, and watched him watching her – she'd forgotten how his fascination appealed to her. 'Aren't you going to ask me to sit down?'

'Do you want to sit down?'

'Of course. It's what I'm here for.'

'Let's go and sit down, then,' he said, and they walked together through the empty tables and past the deserted dance-floor.

He sat with his back to the room, and she saw his shock, quickly suppressed, as Karl appeared directly behind him. The little waiter walked as silently as a cat. 'Would you like to see the champagne menu, sir?'

'No need. We'll have what we had last time. The Lanson.'

'Very good, sir. I shall bring it over to your table at once.'

When Karl had gone, she leaned closer to Terry across the table. 'Where are you from?'

She anticipated a predictable litany of place-names and dates but, for the second time in their acquaintance, he surprised her. A hunted expression came to his pale eyes. 'A long way from here.'

'But you came here,' she said. 'Why?'

'To escape.'

'From what?'

'Everything.'

Again, the sense of something she hadn't seen before – a raw note in the voice, hinting at things he kept hidden from the world. It intrigued her. They were alike on some level he hadn't registered yet. Karl set champagne in an ice-bucket on the table between them, and poured two glasses before he walked away.

She picked up her glass and sipped, avid to begin the interrogation again and get some clue as to what he was concealing. 'Escaping from your wife?'

He looked startled. 'How do you know I'm married?'

'How do you think?' She laughed, delighted by his surprise, and traced over his wedding ring with a long dark-painted nail. 'It's not invisible.' She watched him, unblinking. 'Tell me about your wife. I want to know about her.'

'What do you want to know?'

'What's her name?'

For a second, she thought he wasn't going to answer her. 'Julia,' he said quietly. 'Julia Fielding.'

The moment's pause would normally have made her suspect a lie, but the words came out with conviction. She spoke again, quickly, not giving him time to think. 'What colour hair's she got?'

'Blonde. Her eyes are grey.'

'What does she do for a living?'

'She's a housewife.'

Faster, faster. 'What's her star-sign?'

'Pisces.'

Word-association now, quick-fire. 'What's she like?'

'She's a bitch.'

Silence fell between them, underscored by the escalating noise from the club, the music growing louder around them, a solitary dancer gyrating on the dance-floor. Rosina sat and looked at him, satisfied to have struck a nerve, to get some hint of what really drove him. 'But you're faithful to her,' she said quietly. 'Why?'

'I don't know. *I don't know.*'

Was she making him angry? A part of her wanted to press on and see what the rage in his voice would lead to, but she knew that would be a mistake. It was too soon for that. They sat together, not speaking, for some time. Lights from the disco globe spun around them, turning the champagne in their glasses from red to silver to gold.

'Do you want to leave with me again tonight?' she asked at last.

'Of course I do. You know I do.'

'But you don't want sex.' The trapped look in his eyes brushed her deep inside with the excitement of power. 'Is that really all you want? Just to talk?'

'*Yes.*'

In the drifting languor of the music, she sat and smiled at him. Like hell he didn't want sex, she thought. He *was* a liar, if only to himself. But she'd show him the truth in time, and he'd enjoy it, just as Christine had enjoyed it all those years ago. Her smile widened. 'Well,' she said, 'we'd better drink up.'

They drank. He paid the bill and left the table. She met him outside the shop window five minutes later, and they walked together through the night.

34

I forgot, Terry had said last night. *I didn't know where you were. I was worried.*

But he'd sounded more than worried, and the near-hysterical note in his voice had rung in Marie's mind all day. Along with so much else. His fearful eyes in the study. His preoccupied silences . . .

Her key turned in the front door to darkness. She hurried into the kitchen and put on the light and the radio. Then she went back out into the hallway, took off her coat, put down her handbag, stood for some time, steeling herself inside for what she'd known all day she'd have to do.

She took a deep breath, went to the study and let herself in.

The light from the hallway gave a thin ghostly glow, and provided just enough illumination for her to locate and switch on the desk lamp. A neat circle of white light showed up everything she needed to see. A perfectly normal picture. An old, rarely used computer on one side of a wide dark-wood desk with four drawers beneath it. There was nothing to be afraid of, she told herself, she just needed to know. Her hand moved towards the handle of the first drawer up, touched it – then froze.

He could be back any minute, she thought, God knows how he'll react if he finds me going through his things – but instantly recognised the excuse for what it was. She knew that she was alone and unobserved, and that she would be for some time. But she didn't want to face the real reason for her hesitation. She didn't want to open those drawers because she was scared of what she might find.

In the eye-dazzling lamplight, the realization felt like a hard blow to the stomach; she tried to flinch away from it, but that was impossible. There was no question that she'd sensed dark things lurking in the corners of her marriage before – the time he'd *snapped* at her, the look in his eyes when she'd happened to mention his late mother or murdered sister – but they'd been formless, easy to ignore. Now, though, curiosity forced her to grit her teeth and face them directly in clear daylight, and what she saw appalled her.

Because what she saw was nothing.

After eight years of marriage she didn't know a thing about her husband. It was impossible and ridiculous, but it was also true. Beyond the kind of facts you'd find on a CV or a passport, beyond the simple truths of his sister's murder and his mother's death and his late father's employment as a vicar, there'd never been anything but a series of straightforward adjectives: handsome, reliable, good-natured, caring. Back when their marriage had been comfortable and effortless, she'd found it easy to ignore how little of himself he gave away, so easy that she'd never even known she *was* ignoring it. But now all that was changing . . .

Marie's hand lifted off the drawer handle and fell to her side. She stared blankly at the drawers. She wanted to know what was in there, but she *didn't* want to know. As she began to understand that, behind his eyes and smile, her husband was a stranger to her, the idea of opening the desk drawers frightened her like a high, unshielded ledge.

I can't, she thought – and at that second the phone rang in the hallway.

35

'Marie,' he said, 'it's me.'

Terry stood by the payphone in the starkly lit hotel foyer. Although Rosina was waiting some distance away, he spoke quietly. He didn't want her to hear him calling his wife by her real name. *Why did you say she was called Julia, Terry?* He didn't know. It didn't matter. There was no time to think about that, now.

Down the line, he heard Marie take a long, deep breath. When she spoke, he thought how distant she sounded. How uncharacteristically wary.

'Where are you?' she asked.

'At work. Where else? I told you I'd be late.'

'Oh, yes.' She sounded as if she could hardly bring herself to speak to him – as if part of her hated him. 'What time do you think you'll be back?'

'I don't know. In a couple of hours.'

'I'll probably have gone to bed by then. There's some dinner in the oven.'

'Well,' he said numbly, 'I'll see you later, then.'

'All right.' She hung up.

Terry replaced the receiver and walked back to Rosina. It occurred to him that Marie hadn't once used his name during their brief conversation. *Déjà vu* hit him, and he wished he didn't know why.

Julia. Julia Fielding.

'Did you tell her you'd be late home?' she asked him, as he approached her.

'Yeah.'

'What did she say?'

'Nothing much.' The lift was still broken. They started up the stairs side by side, not touching. 'I don't think she really cares.'

Upstairs, their room was both different and identical: tiny changes in geography and size only confirmed that all the rooms here were the same.

She walked over to the bed and sat down. 'Do you still just want to talk?'

He could imagine too clearly how her skin would feel beneath his hands – smooth and impossibly fine, like raw silk. It was an effort to speak. 'Yes.'

'Even though she doesn't really care?'

Cool raw silk. The imagined magic of her textures. 'Yes.'

'What do you want to talk about?'

'You. Of course.'

She watched him for a few moments. Far away, an ambulance howled like a cat in the night. 'What do you want to know?'

'Tell me about your parents,' he said.

Her face was impassive. 'What do you want to know?'

'Just . . . what they were like.'

'Smug,' she said. 'Stupid.'

He thought of Paul and Julia Fielding, tried to banish their image from his mind. 'You sound like you hate them.'

'I do. Always did.' She gazed across the room with the thoughtful, abstracted expression of an earnest child. 'I'd known they were fakes ever since I was tiny. I was nine when I realised for sure.'

'How?'

'I walked in on my mother one day. She was having sex with the gardener.'

At first he was sure she was joking, then he wasn't. 'What happened?'

'They thought I was in the garden. My father was at work. He was always at work.' The words should have been bitter, but came out with her usual half-amusement. 'They must have been in a hurry to get at each other. They left the bedroom door ajar.'

'And?'

'Nothing. They didn't see me. I went back downstairs.' She said casually, as if on an afterthought, 'Of course, I blackmailed her afterwards.'

He honestly thought he'd misheard. 'What?'

'Oh, not *professionally*. Not with notes or anything.'

There was, he thought, something uniquely decadent about her musing expression, her smooth white brow furrowing in thought. 'But next time I was alone with her, I said she'd left her bedroom door open that afternoon. You should have seen her face.'

He was aware of every breath he took. 'What did you ask for?'

'More pocket money, of course. *Doubled* it,' she said. 'I

don't know why I bothered, really. I always had enough. But it was fun.'

'That's nasty.'

'I know. That's why it was fun.' She was matter-of-fact, businesslike. 'I got a lot worse than that, though, when I got older.'

He stared at her. 'What's the worst thing you ever did?'

'That would have been when I was about fifteen. With a girl I knew from school.'

'What happened with her?'

She went on as though she had not heard him. 'Her name was Christine. I could have talked her into anything.'

A strange edge to her voice promised a revelation, and he waited for her to continue. When she didn't, he couldn't stop himself demanding, 'And?'

She sighed. 'You ask too many questions. You really do. I'll tell you some other time. I'm tired of talking, now.'

He watched her with a kind of reverence: how heartless she was, how untroubled by any considerations save entertainment and *ennui*. In the shadowy half-light, he found himself wondering exactly how it would feel to bond flesh with that heartlessness and become a temporary part of it, and whether her cool and half-amused cruelty would extend into the sexual act itself.

'I have to go,' he said abruptly. 'I have to go home.'

36

It amazed him that it was only half past nine. More than ever, he felt that his time with Rosina had been spent in a different dimension, where the hours that ruled the office and the kitchen stretched and contracted like elastic, and certainties faded into nothing.

He walked out of the hotel foyer into the rainy night and

headed for Victoria station, feeling her magic fade with every step he took. By the time the station was in sight, the stark anxieties of his life had closed in again – the redundancies, Katie, Marie's distance on the phone, a world in which he was becoming less and less important.

The voice returned insidiously, murmuring in his mind. *You said your wife was called Julia*, it reminded him. *You didn't tell Marie about your inheritance. And you don't know why, do you, Terry? You haven't got the slightest idea.*

A wizened elderly man looking at Katie across a little newsagent's shop. Nine-year-old Terry watching him watching her. Something nasty about the old man's scrutiny, something furtive. It was one of the few things Terry ever told his mother about.

But you didn't know why you told her then, either. Even though you could see exactly why, later on. Admit it, Terry. You were on autopilot then. And you're going the same way now—

On the train to Streatham Hill, he gazed out of the window, trying not to hear the insinuating voice. Advertising billboards gave way to tall office blocks and the occasional illuminated window held nothing but a bleak and infinite loneliness. It seemed no time at all before he was getting off at his station and walking the few streets home, rain pattering around him with an empty sound that echoed in his mind.

Part of him had known the lights would all be off when he reached home, and they were. He let himself in, closed, locked and bolted the door behind him. He hung his coat where he always did, and ascended the stairs quietly. The open bedroom door showed Marie lying between the sheets, shadowy but visible in the near-darkness. Something in the quality of the silence felt wrong, unreal.

Was she just pretending to be asleep so she wouldn't have to talk to him tonight?

No. Like the little voice that reminded him of everything he most wanted to forget, the idea was too horrific to be entertained. He went to the bathroom, washed his face, brushed his teeth, and looked at his reflection. The eyes that looked back at him contained an expression at once ambiguous and familiar. He'd seen it many times before, back at the vicarage he'd called home. Fear and the beginning of something else.

Is it anger, Terry? Is it the old anger?

No. It was nothing like that. The dark, secret places in his mind had been sealed off twenty-seven years ago. There was nothing to be afraid of inside, now.

Or so he told himself.

But that night, lying beside his wife in the darkness, he had the terrible dream for the first time.

Book Two

1

It was bizarre, Marie thought, that the stranger things became, the more normally she felt compelled to behave. She'd never felt more alienated from her husband; she'd never fussed around him so brightly in the morning, smiling like a latter-day Doris Day. It seemed to be her way of reassuring herself, distancing herself from the night before. If she could make him coffee and set it down in front of him and talk of domestic banalities, perhaps everything could be seen as business-as-usual.

'Sorry if I was a bit off when you called last night, Terry. I was in a funny mood.'

'I know. It's all right.'

He sounded more than preoccupied this morning – he sounded tired. His pale, shadowed face and dark-circled eyes made her wonder if he'd returned to the study last night when she'd been asleep. An image of the closed desk drawers filled her mind, and when she spoke, her voice sounded false to her own ears, like a bad actress in a too-cosy sitcom. 'Did you sleep all right last night? You look exhausted.'

'Fine.' His voice and expression were inexplicably defensive, and he rose quickly from his seat. 'Well,' he said, 'suppose I'd better be getting on.'

'All right,' she said, in the same sitcom-wife voice. 'Have a nice day at work.' But he left the house without speaking another word.

Alone in the kitchen, she washed up his cup. She was dressed for work already. In the hallway, she clipped her hair back neatly in front of the mirror, and was forcing herself to think about nothing when the phone rang by her hand.

She picked up the receiver. 'Hello?'

'All right, Marie? It's me.'

'Allie.' It was like the return of bright light and normality – she spoke with delight. 'How's it going?'

'All right. Listen, I can't talk long. I just called to ask, do you mind having Lisa again this weekend?'

'Couse not. You know I don't.'

'Great. I'm doing Pontin's again,' said Allie. 'Come round on Saturday morning, yeah? I'll tell you all about it.'

'Sure thing,' said Marie, and they exchanged goodbyes and hung up.

Marie looked in the mirror one last time, and tried to forget about Terry. For as long as she could forget about him, things didn't seem so bad. During the brief bus-ride that took her to the tube station, she thought about gossip with Allie, Lisa's bedtime story and a pleasant private office of her own. In her mind, she held her husband's image at bay, forcing it back like a dangerous animal.

2

When Terry got into the office, Rodge wasn't in. Rob and Christian were talking quietly with Alex on the other side of the room.

'Morning,' said Terry cheerily, but no one seemed to hear him, and his brief semblance of good humour collapsed at once into despair. He was middle-aged, frightened and exhausted. He'd woken at three a.m. with a rusty scream in his throat, and hadn't been able to get back to sleep.

That appalling dream. It whispered in his mind.

He sat down at his computer and switched it on. For once the radio was off, and he could hear the voices across the office quite clearly. 'Well, fucking hell,' Christian was saying. 'You've got to be winding us up.'

'No. Swear to God. Went out with Gavin the other night.

He told me all about it,' said Alex. 'All the suits had a formal meeting the other day. There's going to be redundancies all the way through the company.'

'So how come Viv hasn't said anything?' asked Rob.

'Hasn't said anything *yet.* Don't mean he's not going to, does it? Reckon we'll have a meeting before the end of the day. Now they've told the suits, they've got to tell us.'

'Suppose they have,' said Christian. 'Well, fucking hell.'

So it was true, Terry thought. He didn't know why their words should frighten him further – he'd heard the account handlers in the kitchen – but they did. He felt like an animal in a trap, listening to the slow approach of the hunter's boots. 'Best start getting our CVs together, hey?' said Rob, and laughter resonated across the office, young, confident, maddeningly unafraid.

A few minutes later Rodge came in, called out to Rob and Christian as he always did. 'How's it going, lads?' he asked. 'Looking forward to the awards tonight?' They barely looked round. 'Morning, Terry,' he continued, sitting down at his computer. 'What a night I had last night. Feel like a piece of shit.'

Terry wanted to tell Rodge about what he'd heard, but something stopped him. Rob, Christian and Alex might overhear, and it was too easy to imagine the little clique smirking at each other with the cruelty of the secure. 'Go anywhere good?'

'Just down my local. Me and the lads.' Rodge smiled expansively before lapsing into silence. He got out the latest issue of *Campaign* and started to read it. Across the room, Rob, Christian and Alex were still talking. 'Reckon Pete Mitchell and Pete Carter are going to clean up tonight,' Rob was complaining. 'With that fucking *hedgehog* campaign of theirs. Couple of arrogant pricks.'

'You picked your tux up yet?'

'No. This lunchtime. I'm changing in the bogs here. Haven't got time to go home and back and . . .'

Be rational, Terry, the little voice murmured in his head.

That was you *once,* you *sounded like that once.* But even though Terry knew it was true, he couldn't quite believe it. In the here and now, he'd always been coming up to his tenth birthday and sitting alone at the front of the class, feeling the beginnings of hatred for a world that locked him out. Listening to the carefree hard lads talking among themselves . . .

'That old Harkness,' one of them had said, one bright, sunny, agonising morning. 'He gives me the creeps. Reckon he's a pervert . . .'

Terry cut off the thoughts sharply and brought his attention back to his work. He didn't want to think of anything that might lead on to the memory of Katie lying dead. This morning, it seemed dangerous. He sat and worked in silence for some time, words unravelling across the screen. Beyond the window, the day was pallid and melancholy, and when the radio came on, bittersweet old love songs reminded him of too much.

At half eleven, Sacker came out of his office. 'Everyone got a few minutes?' he asked. 'Just a quick meeting in my office, boys and girls. Won't take long.'

Terry knew it would be about the redundancies, and it was. When they were gathered together in Sacker's chaotic inner sanctum, Sacker spoke quietly and seriously. 'Now, some of you may have been hearing rumours that we're going to have to let some people go. I'm afraid I can't exactly nip them in the bud, much as I'd like to, so I thought it was only fair to have a little get-together. Just so we all know where we stand.' His long pale hands stirred gracefully, in an eloquent simulation of empathy. 'Hopefully I'll be able to cast a little more light on the situation in our Monday meeting but, at this moment in time, I must confess I don't know a great deal more than you do.'

The hunter's boots drawing closer – the trapped, animal terror of helplessness. In the back of his mind, Terry heard Rosina's laughter. He wanted to go back to the club that night more intensely than he could remember wanting anything in his life, but he knew he couldn't. Not two nights running. If Marie wasn't suspicious already, she would be then.

He was cheating on her, in some way.

He realised that now.

3

Marie sat in her new office. While it was much nicer than the bleak open-plan room she was used to – bright, warm, private, crowded with neatly stacked files and pot-plants – she didn't feel comfortable here today. The photograph of Terry that she kept by the computer kept intruding on her peripheral vision as she worked, looming in the corner of her eye, reminding her of everything she wanted most to forget. His pale closed-off eyes. Her fear. The study.

But she pushed away the images as hard as she could. She didn't want to think about them – not here, not now, not ever.

At lunchtime, she left the building, and went to get a quick bite to eat at the bagel bar round the corner. As she joined the queue, she saw that Robert was already in it, the last person in line. 'Hi, Robert,' she said behind him.

He turned, at first surprised, then smiling. 'Afternoon, Marie. Have a good time at the party the other night?'

'Fairly,' she said cautiously. 'I didn't stay that late.'

'Always wise, on a Wednesday night.' He reached the front of the queue, ordered his lunch and took the proffered bag. 'Well, see you later.'

She'd have liked to talk for longer, but he was already walking out into the street. She ordered her own lunch on a tray to eat in. Sitting by the window, she munched and watched the steady ebb and flow of passing strangers. It was a shame, she thought, that her conversations with Robert were always over so quickly. Their brief exchanges had told her that he was someone she could really talk to, relate to, understand.

Not like Terry, she thought, then brushed the idea away, horrified. She finished her lunch, and went back to work.

The rest of her afternoon passed rapidly. She finished her three-hour review of the target figures, and held a brief meeting to remind the Credit team that they had two new people starting on Monday. When they'd all left and she was alone in her office, her eyes settled again on the photo of Terry. It was a blurred, poor-quality snapshot, but her mind gave it an extra dimension that unsettled her. Suddenly, she sensed nothing behind his warm smile – it was as if he'd been photographed wearing a mask.

At a quarter to seven, she shut down her computer and headed for the lifts. In the institutional emptiness of the hallway, she saw Sandra waiting, too. They smiled at each other, slightly awkwardly.

'You been working late, too?' asked Sandra.

'My normal hours now, worse luck.' It had always been easy to talk to Sandra in what she already thought of as the old days, and she was surprised to find that it still was. 'You really don't want to get promoted.'

'My bank manager might like it if I was.' They laughed together. The lift arrived, and they got in. 'Hardly saw you at the party the other night,' Sandra continued. 'Mind you, me and Cheryl and Kim went on to Jacomo's Bar quite early on. Don't think any of us felt too good the morning after.'

'Wish I could have come with you.' The lift stopped and the doors slid open. They walked out of Reception together into the dark night. 'But I suppose it's like you said to me a while back. Not *professional*.'

'Not at *work*, maybe, Marie, but it's stupid if we have to stop being friendly because you've been promoted.' They walked past kebab shops, newsagents and restaurants. Sandra looked at Marie quizzically. 'Why don't we meet up over the weekend or something? Sunday lunch?'

'I'd love to, but I'm looking after my niece this weekend.'

'So? I'll have Derek and the kids in tow. We could all go for lunch together. Make a change from cooking at home.'

'Well . . .' Marie wanted to, badly. Her only real reservation was Terry. He'd never shown any interest in meeting her friends, or introducing her to his. *But why not?* she thought, with sudden irritation. If he doesn't need something to take him out of himself, I don't know who does. 'Sure,' she said. 'That'd be great.'

On the way to the tube station, they sorted out the details, and settled on a nice pub Sandra knew in Clapham, half-way between their homes. Past the ticket barriers, their paths diverged. 'Well, see you Sunday, then, Marie,' said Sandra. 'Have a good night.' Marie waved and stepped on to the escalator for the Northern line, and tried to lose her fast-growing worries in the prospect of Sunday lunch.

4

What on earth could Terry be thinking of recently when the silences stretched out in the kitchen and he didn't seem to notice them? Marie wished she knew. Perhaps he thought of work, but she had no real idea what his work involved. Try as she might, she couldn't picture his office or his daily schedule. As they ate, the silence hung around them, and she felt she had to speak. 'Why don't you ever talk about your job any more, Terry?'

'What do you want to know?'

'I don't know.' But she did. After a few seconds she pressed on, with the impulsiveness of desperation. 'What you did today. What you talked about in the office. What your boss said to you.'

'What makes you think my boss said anything to me today?'

She didn't understand why he sounded so defensive. The bewilderment, fear and irritation that were becoming her constant companions rose in her throat like bile. 'There's no need to *snap*. I was just *asking*.'

'Well, there's nothing to tell. Everything's fine. The office is fine. I'm fine. Don't you think I'd tell you if anything was wrong?'

She wanted to lie, but somehow couldn't bring herself to. 'I don't know. You've been in such a weird mood lately, I don't know *what* to think, any more.'

'So you think I'd lie? You've really lost that much trust in me?'

His voice was reasonable on the surface, but it held an undercurrent of something both distant and terribly close, trembling on the edge of tears. He'd been the same way, she remembered, after the doctor had broken the news of his infertility – on the night he'd *snapped* at her – and she backed down fast. 'Of course not, love. You know I trust you. I was just curious, that's all.'

He didn't answer. Silence fell again. It was appalling, Marie felt, to see this absolute impasse as a kind of refuge, to sense that there was something far worse than sitting in the claustrophobic night, feeling a familiar well-lit kitchen become an emotional no man's land. When she spoke again, it was with genuine urgency, a need to expand this closed, unsettling world they shared and bring in other people.

'I said we'd have Sunday lunch with a friend of mine from work. Me and you and Lisa. We're meeting her and her husband and kids in the Red Lion, in Clapham. It'll be fun.'

'All right,' he said quietly. 'Whatever you like.'

Marie knew she should have been relieved that he'd agreed but, if anything, her fears intensified. Something in the quality of his silence was all wrong, and while his eyes were fixed on the food he ate, she sensed he wasn't seeing it. A secret world existed behind his expressionless face, a world she didn't understand, and never had. She remembered the closed drawers in the study, and shivered inside.

They went to bed at half past ten. She used the bathroom first. When he came into the bedroom, she pretended to be asleep. She couldn't bear him to touch her somehow. Not tonight.

5

Rosina couldn't sleep. Far away, a siren howled through the night. She lay awake in the Escape-scented darkness and listened to it die away. Try as she might, she felt ill at ease, and longed for the return of cold, solid certainties.

You're never scared of anything, are you, Rosina?

Why should I be? There's nothing to be scared of, Chris.

Back then, she remembered, there'd been nothing but certainties. They'd often been cruel but they'd always existed: the permanency of the white-and-pinewood bedroom and the beautiful three-storey house in Chelsea, the elegant parents who smiled out from the silver frame. Rosina had never consciously thought it back then, but now she saw that she'd always assumed life would stay like that. No matter what was said or done.

Do you know, I blackmailed my mother when I was a little girl?

No. I don't believe you.

It's true. I caught her screwing the gardener when I was about nine. Told her I'd tell Daddy, if she didn't double my pocket money.

And she did it?

Of course she did it, Chris. People always do what I want.

Yes, Rosina remembered, the rules of the world had been carved in stone back then: a cold dark leader and a silly little blonde who always did as she was told. Even though she'd always secretly hated Christine, she now missed the way it had been in those days, before it had all gone wrong. No unspeakable secrets had hidden behind her eyes then – there hadn't been anything she couldn't confess, if she wanted to.

Not like now. She'd come too far to turn back now.

Alone in the darkness, the world melted around her, and the secrets of her life stepped out from the shadows; in a locked box on her dressing-table, the things she couldn't possibly tell

Terry about. The stark facts that would drive him away. She wasn't the woman he thought she was: there were dark corners that he didn't understand. And, suddenly, her usual pleasure in secrecy took on new shades of fear and loneliness, and the ambiguities that surrounded her took on the edge of a nightmare.

I walked in on my mother one day, she'd said, *having sex with the gardener*, and the memory of her own voice alarmed her. She'd told him so much, she thought – she'd told him nothing.

No way of turning back now. She pressed her face into the pillow, inhaling Escape for long, slow, calming seconds. It was the same perfume that had touched the air back in that white-and-pinewood bedroom, that coloured all her memories of that time. It made her feel better. She'd be herself again tomorrow night, because then she'd be back in the club, and in the club you could be anyone you wanted.

Sleep drifted in slowly. Behind her closed eyelids, disco lights spun across a silver-framed photograph, and red neon and darkness showed through a bedroom window, and then and now blurred into one.

6

'And they're giving me a permanent contract there,' said Allie cheerfully. 'They told me last Sunday. Saturday and Sunday nights for the whole of next month.'

It was a great effort for Marie to sound involved and happy. 'That's fantastic, Allie. I'm really pleased for you.'

'You don't sound it.' Allie looked at her closely. 'What's the matter? You seem a bit worried.'

Marie wanted to tell her everything was fine, but it was impossible to lie with Allie's sceptical gaze fixed on her. 'Well, if you really want to know, it's Terry.'

'Terry? What about him?'

'That's just it. I don't know.' A brief silence fell in the brightly decorated living room. She struggled to collect her thoughts, express them coherently. 'He's been acting so strangely, Allie. I can't tell you.'

Allie's forehead corrugated. 'How do you mean?'

'Just—' Marie took a deep breath. 'It's as if he's thinking about something else all the time. And I haven't got a clue what it could be.' She expected the words to come out with the sinister edge they'd acquired in her mind, but as she spoke, she realised their inadequacy: they were so simple and straightforward, that they sounded as if her husband might be concealing some harmless little secret.

When Allie spoke, she sounded surprised and reassuring, as if she had no idea why her normally level-headed sister should be worrying. 'Maybe he's got problems at work or something. You're always saying he works hard.'

'It's not that simple. I know it's not.' She spoke abruptly – too abruptly. 'I'm sorry, Allie, it's just – I think he might be having some kind of breakdown.'

'*Terry?*' Allie spoke his name with incredulity. 'Oh, Marie, you really *have* to be joking. I can't see that for a moment.'

Allie's certainty did nothing to reassure Marie: she was aware of how little Allie had seen of him, how misleading the images in her sister's mind were. A calm, smiling, amiable figure at Lisa's christening, at their parents' golden wedding anniversary party, at family Christmases. As Marie had realised, she knew him little better than her sister did – but she could see now that there was far more to him than the façade implied.

And even the façade's crumbling now, she thought. If Allie met him today, she might just see what I'm talking about. The idea should have pleased her, but it disturbed her even more. Much as she wanted to be understood, she didn't want anyone to notice his strangeness for themselves.

'Well,' she said, reconciling herself to secrecy, 'maybe you're right.'

After that, there didn't seem to be anything much to say.

Allie talked a bit more about her singing, but it was as if she'd been infected by Marie's tension: her usual *joie de vivre* seemed muted. It was rare for silences to fall when they were alone together, but they did that morning. To Marie, it was a relief when Lisa came into the living room with her overnight bag, and she could rise from her seat with a semblance of briskness, and say that they'd better be getting on.

7

Terry was fading out. At least, that was how it felt. As if he constantly became a little more insubstantial, a little less visible. He could feel people look through him, so that he had to remind them he was there. It was the way he'd started to feel shortly before his tenth birthday.

Only Lisa still seemed to see him clearly, and he found her scrutiny more uncomfortable than anything. More than ever, he thought that she saw too much.

'I wonder what Sandra's husband's going to be like,' Marie said on Saturday night, after she'd put Lisa to bed. 'She's never really talked about Derek.'

It should have comforted him that she spoke to him, but it didn't. He could tell she didn't really want his feedback, just needed someone to bounce her own bright, distant concerns off – she'd say exactly the same things to her sister, her friends, anyone. 'She's got two kids, you know,' she said. 'They'll be there tomorrow. They're both about Lisa's age.'

He didn't answer: she didn't seem to expect him to. Sitting beside her on the sofa, he experienced a wave of nostalgia for the days when he'd been important to her. Recently she, too, seemed to see too much – and to care too little. He wasn't sure whether she suspected the truth of his failure in the office or not. Perhaps, after all, she did.

She doesn't know about your inheritance, Terry, a little voice whispered. *Or Rosina. Or even what really happened to Katie—*

The voice was becoming harder to get rid of. Once, he'd been able to silence it at will; now, he could only turn it down to a semi-audible murmur. But he tried to shut it off just the same. It was terrible to hear it muttering behind the three-dimensional television noise, as he sat in the familiar living-room, beside his wife of eight years. It was like having an enemy locked up in his head.

You should know what that *feels like, Terry*, the voice whispered again, and he flinched inside, because Marie was sitting next to him, and whatever Marie thought she suspected, he knew that she really suspected less than nothing. The truth wouldn't occur to her . . .

He desperately wanted to be alone, but the idea of going into the study had become unbearable to him. Once, he'd felt as if he needed reminding of the past and its secrets – now he had to guard against them – but not any more. He remembered them only too vividly, and all he wanted was to forget.

That night, he had the dream for a second time, or at least part of it. He woke up half-way through it, wrenched out of sleep with a thin cry, heart thumping erratically in his chest. He sat up in bed and looked down at his sleeping wife, wondering what she'd think if she knew what the dream had involved. If she knew how his subconscious mind was beginning to tempt him.

She'd care about that, Terry. She'd care about that.

He was afraid to go back to sleep for fear that the dream would pick up where it had left off. He lay beside Marie, and thought about Rosina, the sound of her laughter, the imagined silken texture of her skin. Her image, inexplicably, was calming, soothing him like the prospect of salvation, and when exhaustion finally overcame him, he dreamed of nothing worse than a sunny orchard.

On Sunday morning the bathroom mirror told him that the sleepless hours had taken their toll: he looked drained and shadowed, paler than ever. He showered, shaved, dressed and brushed his teeth, then went downstairs to the kitchen. Marie and Lisa were eating breakfast at the kitchen table.

'Morning,' he said, with a brightness he didn't feel, and was reminded of his mornings in the office. Out of the window, he saw it was raining again. 'What a day.'

'Hope it perks up later,' said Marie. 'We're meeting Sandra and Derek at two, remember? You want a coffee?'

'Thanks.' He sat down at the table, feeling fear, lethargy and despair blend into a single emotion, remembering what the day had in store. He'd had Sunday lunch with strangers before when he'd been fading out. Sunday lunch with people who hadn't cared at all. Because they were friends of his mother.

Julia Fielding.

8

They were called the Wilsons, he remembered. Of course, he hadn't known their first names. He, his mother, father and Katie had gone to their house for Sunday lunch, when he'd been ten for almost a week. They'd talked to his parents, and fussed over little Katie, but they hadn't noticed him. They'd seemed to look right through him.

'You must be Derek,' said Marie, smiling across the table as the newcomers sat down. 'This is Terry, my husband, and my niece Lisa.'

'I'm Sandra,' said the little blonde woman, taking Terry's hand briefly. 'Pleased to meet you. These two here are Lee and Jessica.'

Terry saw two sullen-faced children who looked about eight and nine. He smiled at them, and they stared back with bored, indifferent eyes. The pub was vaguely upmarket, ostentatiously olde worlde – dark wood and framed Guinness posters gleamed around couples and families, and lounging groups of twentysomething friends. Beyond the windows, the day looked like an overcast evening. 'How old are you, then, love?' Sandra asked Lisa.

Lisa looked at the table. 'Six.'

'She's a bit shy, bless her,' said Marie. 'Especially with grown-ups she doesn't know.'

'They're all the same at that age,' said Sandra. 'Jessica was, anyway. She's nine, now. Lee's eleven.'

'Don't know where the time went,' said Derek, and he, Sandra and Marie laughed. Terry tried to join in, but in his own ears his laughter sounded false. He felt as if he'd barged in on a group of old friends who were strangers to him. 'I was saying to Marie a few weeks ago,' Sandra said to Derek, 'how quickly they seem to have grown up. Doesn't seem five minutes, I said, since I was changing their nappies.'

'We've got those new people starting on Monday, haven't we?' Marie said to Sandra. 'I'm not looking forward to showing them the ropes.'

'Don't blame you,' said Sandra. 'Well, suppose we'd better have a look at the menu. I'm starving.'

Terry had never felt less like eating in his life. A queasy feeling in the pit of his stomach told him that every mouthful was going to be an effort. For the sake of appearances, though, he had to pretend to be hungry. He went for roast beef and Yorkshire pudding, as they all did, and Derek went to the bar to put their food order in.

Sandra and Marie talked about work, about people named Cheryl and Martin and Carol Ellis, and Sandra's children bickered between themselves. Terry sat alone, unnoticed, apparently invisible. As though a sound dial was slowly turning in his head, the noise around him grew louder. Sandra's shrieking laughter and the chatter of four girls at the next table and the endless background noise from the bar closed in on him, underscored by the empty, somehow tragic sound of the rain. Across the table, he saw Lisa's eyes fixed on him, and knew that she understood everything. Cold sweat broke out on his forehead. 'Just going to the loo,' he said, rising from the table. 'Back in a minute.' But Marie was engrossed in her conversation with Sandra, and neither heard him.

In the well-scrubbed desolation of the gents', he locked himself into a cubicle. Once more, he remembered Julia Fielding, Katie, a couple called the Wilsons who'd invited them to lunch before it had all come crashing down. The slow, agonising birth of hatred. Suddenly Rosina alone stood between him and absolute terror. For several minutes, he sat motionless, trying not to think about the dream he'd had last night. A high, steady, keening noise echoed somewhere inside his head, behind the thudding of his heart, and the escalating rain on the frosted-glass window.

9

'Well,' said Marie, 'that was nice, wasn't it?'

They'd got the bus back from Clapham and were now walking home, huddled together under Terry's large umbrella. Despite herself, Marie had felt a sense of loss as she'd said goodbye to Sandra and Derek. After the easy, cheerful chat over good pub food, after the gossip about Cheryl's husband and the management team and how much commission the sales team were making came *this* – the hard rain pattering on the umbrella to become the only sound in the world, Lisa walking beside her with her eyes cast down, Terry's silence. It was four thirty in the afternoon, and already getting dark. Bleak empty streets shone with puddles and desolation. She couldn't bear to acknowledge the way she felt, and she'd spoken brightly in the hope of escaping it.

Terry didn't reply, unless his shoulders rising and falling could be taken as an answer. As she watched him walking with his eyes fixed straight ahead, her loneliness snapped into fury. 'Well, was it nice or not? Don't just *shrug* like that.'

'What do you want me to do? What do you want me to say?'

The simmering anger in his voice took her by surprise – something beneath his words sounded almost like hatred. In her mind, she took a fearful step back. 'Just answer me properly,' she said. 'I hate it when you ignore me.'

'Well, that's *something*. I didn't think you felt anything about me any more.'

Normally this would have touched her with guilt and sympathy, but his tone precluded any such emotion. It chilled her like the snarl of a vicious dog. Lisa walked beside them, watching them with detached curiosity. Marie didn't say anything for the rest of the walk home, because she couldn't think of anything to say, and camaraderie in a well-lit lunch-time pub had taken on the shades of an unreachable past.

When they got home, Terry spoke, without looking at her. 'I'll be in the study,' he said. 'I've got some work to do.' Then he was walking down the hallway, and the study door was closing behind him.

She stood looking after him, her heartbeat ticking in her ears until she became aware of Lisa beside her, watching her face with huge grey quizzical eyes. She fought to speak calmly. 'Come into the kitchen, Lisa. Sit down, and I'll make you a milkshake.'

The lights lent a semblance of bright sunlight to the room as she mixed Lisa's drink. The child sat at the table, and silence gathered until it was deafening. When Lisa spoke behind her, Marie jumped.

'Auntie Marie?'

She looked round sharply. 'What is it?'

Lisa's expression was alert and cautious. 'What's wrong with Uncle Terry?'

So others could see it too. There was a hard, uncomfortable lump in Marie's throat. 'Nothing, love.'

Silence closed in again. She finished making Lisa's milk-shake and set it on the table in front of the little girl. Lisa picked it up and sipped it without speaking. Marie went to the window and drew the blinds against the gathering night, hearing the last listless raindrops on the glass, thinking of Terry in the study, looking at things he'd never shown her. That night, she thought, she and her husband would watch TV in the living room and not talk about anything that mattered to them: a man and a woman in a crowded modern capital city, uneasily alone together as if they were marooned at sea.

10

He couldn't sleep. He knew why not: he was too frightened of the dream. Over the last few days, his subconscious had become a vicious stranger, grinning as it lay in wait, ready to ambush him as soon as he closed his eyes. He didn't want another encounter with that horror.

That afternoon in the study, he'd remembered it. Even though he'd only gone in there to be alone, he hadn't been able to stop himself opening the bottom drawer, reliving those early years.

Beside him, Marie stirred. She didn't have anything to say to him any more. After she'd put Lisa to bed, they'd sat up together, watching TV in virtual silence. Her eyes when she looked at him were chilly, irritated, and when she spoke to him, she never used his name.

She'd rather be spending the evening with her friends, Terry. With Sandra and Derek and their kids. You saw how she looked at them. She never looks that way with you, any more . . .

And he knew that she was quickly losing any love for him she might still have, and that when he walked into the office tomorrow, indifferent strangers would look straight through him, and he was going to be made redundant in the near future. And there was nothing he could do about any of it, except stand helplessly by and watch himself fading out. And the worst thing of all was knowing that he'd been here before.

Robert Harkness, Terry. They said the killer's name was Robert Harkness.

He hadn't known the man's first name back then, of course. He'd only discovered that after they'd arrested him. Before Katie's murder, he'd just been old Harkness, a relative newcomer to the small town, a peripheral, slightly unnerving presence. *Old*, they'd all thought him, but it turned out that he'd been a small, stooping, bald forty-seven. A man with no job, who lived alone in a shabby little flat. A rather pathetic figure, Terry remembered, even though he gave you the creeps – a derided and solitary bogeyman.

That old Harkness, the hard lads said. *Reckon he's a pervert.*

Perhaps it was that which had planted the seeds of an idea, Terry thought, that chance snatch of other people's conversation overheard in the classroom. All he knew was that later the same week, when he was in the corner shop with Katie, buying sweets, he'd seen Harkness standing by the magazine racks watching her. And Terry found himself thinking that maybe the hard lads had been right. There was something unpleasant in the man's scrutiny, something furtive. Terry didn't know then why he had to tell his mother about it. He just knew he had to.

Julia Fielding, cooking in the kitchen, looking round with distracted, irritated eyes. 'What do you want? Can't you see I'm busy?'

He had to gather all his courage to continue. 'It's Katie. When we were in the newsagent today. I saw that old man looking at her. That old Harkness.'

Her immediate attention, for once, undivided. 'What do you mean? How was he looking at her?'

'Just . . . funny. I don't know. I just thought you should know . . .'

Terry lay awake in the darkness, remembering it all. How it had felt to sense that he was being driven by something outside himself, beyond himself, the bewilderment of not quite understanding his own motivation. Why had he gone for those long walks after school and told his parents he had extra maths? Why had he told his mother about Harkness looking at Katie? Why had he told the few boys he talked to at school the same thing? But the answer was simple. He didn't know.

Maybe for the same reason why you started going to the club after work. Why you didn't tell Marie about your inheritance. Why you said your wife's name was Julia. The little voice in his head was more disturbing than ever, mocking, insinuating. *Because you were fading out then, Terry. And because you're fading out now . . .*

He didn't want to go to sleep tonight. He didn't want to have the dream again.

But, in the end, sleep and the dream could not be denied.

11

The Monday-morning meeting was held in the seventh-floor boardroom, as it always was. Rob and Christian sat smoking with their feet on the table, flanked by Alex and Lucy. Terry's eyes kept moving over to them – the past incarnate, the unreachable years of success. Friday's awards ceremony had gone well.

'And I'm sure you've all heard about our *triumph* at Grosvenor House,' Sacker was saying chummily. 'Best Poster Campaign of the Year, no less. Rob and Christian, *congratulations*.'

A smattering of applause. Rob and Christian's good-natured, arrogant eyes panned round the table. 'Pete Mitchell and Pete Carter can kiss our fucking *arse*,' said Rob, and Christian said, 'They know where they can stick their fucking *hedgehog*,' and Sacker led the laughter like a conductor, long white elegant hands rising, stirring, falling again for silence.

'And, of course, Alex and Lucy are to be *much* congratulated. Second place in Press Ad of the Year's not to be sniffed at, as I'm sure we all know.' Another short burst of applause –

Terry saw Rodge clapping harder than anyone. This time, Sacker didn't let it go on for quite as long. His palms met with a sharp noise like a gunshot, and the room fell silent.

'Much as I hate to spoil the mood, I'm afraid there are rather less pleasant issues to be discussed. Some things have been clarified over the weekend, so at least we can all know where we stand. Redundancies are to be announced over the next few weeks, and it's *inevitable* that our department's going to be affected. The simple fact of the matter is . . .'

Terry barely heard the rest. Sacker's words blurred around him, turning down to an almost inaudible murmur at the back of his mind. Dark veins pulsed at the outskirts of his vision. If Sacker said a few weeks, he meant a fortnight. Then and there, he knew that he had anything up to two weeks left here.

And what then, Terry? What then? the little voice whispered again, and faded into Sacker's well-modulated tones, which wore emotion the way a catwalk model wore clothes. 'So there it is,' he was saying, 'and I'm afraid there's not a *great* deal else that I can say. So I suppose we should all return our collective nose to the grindstone. There's work to be done out there, boys and girls.'

In the office, Rob and Christian played table-football. The noise was almost drowned by their voices, and Alex and Lucy calling to them: 'Get some work done, you lazy bastards,' howled Alex, 'or they'll chuck you out for doing fuck-all all day.'

'Piss off, Alex. We'll do what we like. You're just jealous.'

'Yeah. Couldn't even get Press Ad of the Year, could you?'

'Well, we can't all be the new David Abbot,' said Lucy archly. 'Starting to go to your head, isn't it? Laugh if they did chuck you out.' Terry heard them with nightmare clarity.

Rob and Christian returned to their desks. 'Have to start getting our portfolios together,' said Rob flippantly, '*and* our CVs if we're not *appreciated* here, you know . . .'

Out of the corner of his eye, Terry saw Rodge rising from his desk, approaching the awards set – it chilled him in a way he couldn't place, like watching a fellow soldier stepping out into no man's land. He perched his portly buttocks on the edge of Christian's desk. 'Going to have to start polishing up our interview skills, aren't we?' he announced jovially. 'Get our best suits ready.'

'You worried, then, Rodge?'

'Fuck off. I'm young, aren't I?' More than ever, Terry saw, Rodge was the brash comedian, but the façade had never rung more pathetically untrue. He got off Christian's desk and moved around with an attempt at Christian's swagger, ponytail swinging like a metronome. 'Plenty of good years in me yet.' And a cold hand gripped down on Terry's heart, because they weren't laughing *with* Rodge: it was crystal clear they were laughing *at* him, and it was equally crystal clear that Rodge didn't know.

'You *sure* you're not worried, Rodge?' asked Alex slyly, and the laughter exploded again as Rodge faced him with a mockery of mock-wrath. Terry felt a sudden stab of hatred for their unthinking insider brutality. It wasn't fair, he thought, to laugh at poor old Rodge and his thinly veiled terror – but it was a hypocritical thought: deep inside he wasn't thinking about Rodge, but about himself.

He sat at his desk, listening to Rodge pretending to be part of a little group that despised him, and felt suddenly that he owed Marie no allegiance. That night, he'd seek out salvation in the club and Rosina, and he'd do what he wanted.

Whatever he wanted.

12

'This is my office – the door's always open. There's a weekly team meeting in here on Fridays, to see where we are and who's doing what. If you have any problems – God forbid – I'm the first person to speak to. Don't stand on formality, just come in and have a word.'

In the big main open-plan office, the two new Credit girls stared back at Marie: one a bored-looking thirtysomething, the other an apprehensive teenager. Their close scrutiny, she supposed, was normal enough for new employees, but it made her feel edgy just the same. She had the feeling that they were seeing through to her true fears – the three hours' sleep last night, the circles under her eyes that Estée Lauder could do only so much to conceal, the deepening awareness of Terry's strangeness.

You're getting as bad as him, she castigated herself. She passed the new girls on to Cheryl, said it was good to have them on board, went into her office. While she had no difficulty concentrating on her work that morning, she felt as if her mind was running on two different tracks at once: the well-lit overground efficiency ran smoothly, subterranean fears rattled through the darkness below.

At lunchtime, she sought out Sandra in the ladies'. She was brushing her hair and met Marie's eyes in the mirror. 'Hi, Marie. That was a nice lunch yesterday. Should do it more often.'

'Good idea.' Marie got a lipstick out of her bag. She paused in the process of reapplying it, aware that there was no subtle way round the question. 'What did you think of Terry?'

'Gorgeous, isn't he?' Sandra replaced her brush in her bag. 'I've got to say, Marie, that photo you've got of him on your desk doesn't do him justice.'

She watched Sandra's face closely for signs of evasion or doubt, but could find none – and she knew Sandra well enough to be sure she wasn't hiding anything. It was strange, for she'd been unsettled that Lisa had noticed something was wrong with her husband, but she was even more unsettled that Sandra apparently hadn't.

'It's okay, Marie,' said Sandra quickly, apparently misunderstanding her silence. 'In case you haven't noticed, I'm stuck with my Derek. Anyway, your Terry's a bit quiet for me.'

Marie pounced on the word like a terrier on a rat. 'How do you mean, quiet?'

'How do you think I mean? Just didn't say much.'

Marie replaced the lid on her lipstick and put it back in her bag.

'You're a bit touchy today,' Sandra went on. 'Is something wrong?'

'It's nothing.' There was, she understood, no way of expressing her anxieties. 'Anyway, I'll see you later. Got to get some lunch.'

When half past six arrived and work was over for the day, Marie switched off her computer and rose from her desk. She told herself she wasn't looking forward to the journey home, but knew that there was more to it than that. She wasn't looking forward to arriving. Out of the lift, she saw that Robert had taken the stairs, and was just coming down the last few. She stopped, smiled, waited for him to catch her up.

'Hello, Marie,' he said, falling into step beside her. 'Mind if I walk with you for a few minutes?'

'Feel free,' she said. 'Which way are you going?'

'I parked just up from the tube station.'

Outside, they walked for a while without speaking. Bright lights from passing cars splashed across the pavement. Beside Robert, Marie felt a tension that was both linked to and entirely separate from her fear of home. She couldn't think of anything to say.

'Listen,' he said abruptly, 'do you want to come for a drink? There's a wine bar I know round the corner. It's a nice place.'

Bright lights, conversation and an attraction that she'd felt for weeks – a way of postponing the inevitability of home. The force of Marie's longing was irresistible. 'All right,' she heard herself say. 'I'd love to.'

13

The club was quiet as it always was at this time. Rosina stood alone by the bar, watching the barman polishing glasses. Before she'd met Terry, she'd never come into work early, but now she always did. She wanted to be there when he entered.

When the bell rang in the club from Reception, she was instantly alert, preparing herself for a group of tourists who'd strayed out of their financial depth, for one of the suave, older men in suits who always put her in mind of a silver frame. But it wasn't any of them. When the red-velvet curtains stirred and parted, it was Terry.

'Hello,' she said, as he drew close.

'Do you want to sit down?'

'Of couse,' she said. 'I *always* want to sit down. You must know that by now.'

At the table, Karl brought over the champagne menu. 'We'll have the Lanson,' said Terry, and Karl walked away. Rosina sat facing the club, watching it slowly grow busier. When Terry spoke, his voice took her by surprise.

'What do you do when you're not here?'

There was something different about him tonight, she thought, something uncharacteristically reckless. But she'd grown adept at hiding her real feelings, and knew the thought didn't show on her face. 'What do you think I do?'

'I don't know,' he said slowly. 'I can't imagine you having a life outside here.'

'Imagine what you like.' For a moment, she felt almost unsettled – she was supposed to know everything about him, but he wasn't supposed to know her. That was how it had always been, how it had been with Christine. 'It doesn't matter. I can be anything you want, in here.'

Silence fell between them, broken by the muted early-evening music. She hid behind her cold, secret smile as he watched her. When Karl came over with the champagne in an ice-bucket, he poured two glasses, stood back, smiled. 'Have a good evening, sir,' he said, then went away.

In the moment that Terry's attention had been distracted Rosina had become flippant and cruel and herself again – she leaned in closer to him. '*You* talk,' she said. 'Tell me things.'

'What sort of things?'

'Anything,' she said. Then, with calculated impulsiveness, 'Tell me about your family.'

'That would be my parents. There wasn't anyone else.'

'Nobody?'

Something had told her that he wasn't telling the whole truth, and she was delighted to see that her instinct was right. His eyes held a trapped look, Christine's look. 'There was my sister. But she died when I was ten.'

'What happened to her?'

'She was in a car crash.'

'What was her name?'

'Lisa.'

Was he being honest now? She couldn't tell. There were deeper layers than she'd expected to find. It intrigued her to think he had secrets. 'You're hiding something from me,' she said coolly. 'I can feel it.'

'I'm not,' he said. '*I'm not.*'

Under the ever-moving points of light that swam across them from the disco globe, she sipped at her champagne and gazed at him. He was beautiful, and he was strange, and the occasional rage she sensed within him drew her more than anything. In his moments of anger he reminded her of herself, as well as of Christine, both the way she was now and a distant, more innocent self. How she'd been before she'd taken on the greatest secret of all.

'*You* talk,' he said abruptly. 'I want to know more about *you.*'

'Not now. At the hotel.' The difference in him tonight made her chance her hand, gamble her cool façade on an instinct. 'Do you still just want to talk to me there?'

'You know I don't,' he said quietly. 'Not tonight.'

There was a note of raw hunger in his voice that thrilled her. She looked past him to where Karl came and went, ferrying champagne in ice-buckets. Life was fun here, she thought, in the thin, rosy lights, as Vicki and the others giggled in sequined dresses and the music murmured sweet nothings to the writhing dancers, and nobody really knew who she was, or what she had to hide. She sat and looked back at Terry's longing, feeling the gradual approach of what she wanted above all: the power to corrupt.

14

'So whereabouts do you live?' asked Robert.

They were sitting in a small pleasant wine bar with long wooden tables, dark brick walls, bottles lined in endless ranks to ceiling height behind the bar. Quiet music played in the background – dinner-party music, middlebrow, unobtrusive. To Marie, it felt like sanctuary: a place without shadows, where she could smile and talk and forget about home.

'Streatham Hill,' she said, sipping her white wine. 'How about you?'

'Islington.'

'Nice area,' she said, 'so I've heard.'

'Handy for work, anyway,' he said. 'I've just got a flat there. Seems ridiculous to have anything bigger, when I'm on my own.'

She couldn't stop herself from asking. 'Not married?'

'Divorced. About seven years ago.' Sympathy dawned in her eyes and she saw him notice it.

'There's nothing to be sorry about, believe me. It's the old cliché, I suppose – we just grew apart.'

'Still,' she said, 'it's a shame.'

'Not at all. We're still in touch. Still friends, even. When she married again a couple of years ago, she invited me to the wedding.'

'Did you go?'

'Of course.'

'Didn't it bother you?'

'No,' he said. 'Should it have?'

How different he was from Terry – despite herself, she couldn't help comparing him to her husband. There was a straightforward quality to him that enraptured her: it was a vision of all she didn't have. 'What do you do when you're not working?' she asked.

Her tone must have implied that he usually *was* working, but he answered as if expressing a simple statement of fact. 'Oh, I'm not a *workaholic.* I like my job, but it's still good to leave at the end of the day.'

'What do you do then?'

'Well, I play a lot of tennis, travel when I can. Go out with friends.' A brief silence fell – they watched each other across the table. 'Don't know what else, really. I used to play in a band in my student days, if that's any use.'

'My sister's into music. She's a singer,' said Marie. 'Well, a sort of singer. There's no way you'd have heard of her.'

'Maybe I will,' he said. 'One day.'

They talked about the music business and university, the office and everything in the world – Marie didn't notice how quickly the time was passing. When she finally glanced at her watch, she was appalled to see that it was almost half past ten. 'Oh, God,' she said. 'I'll have to be getting home. My husband'll be worried.' A brief pause, a moment of subtle embarrassment. 'I'm married, you know,' she added, pointlessly.

'I did.' At first he spoke gently, then briskly. 'Well – d'you want a lift back?'

'Don't be silly. It's miles out of your way. I'll get a taxi.'

'It's no trouble,' he said. 'Really.'

'No, honestly, Robert.' It would feel terrible, she knew, having a dream drive her back to a living nightmare. Much as she wanted to spend more time with him, she knew it was out of the question. 'I'll get a taxi.'

'I'll wait with you,' he said, and they rose from the table, put on their coats, headed out into the night.

It was easy to flag down a cab outside the wine bar. She said a quick goodbye to Robert, climbed in, gave instructions to the driver. Unfamiliar streets unwound endlessly beyond the window, and the landmarks only became familiar a few minutes from home. As she paid off the driver, she saw that there were no lights on in the house. She hurried out of the cab, got her key out of her bag and let herself in.

Even before she'd gone upstairs and seen the double bed still neatly made, she knew that Terry hadn't come home yet – something in the quality of the silence, the air. She checked the answerphone for messages but none had been left. A deep-rooted unease pervaded her mind, painful after the easy pleasure of chatting with Robert. He was probably working late, she thought. If she went straight to bed, he'd be home before long. But the idea didn't feel right. In the bathroom, she washed off her makeup, brushed and flossed her teeth. When she went to bed, the sheets felt cold around her, and she took a long time getting to sleep.

15

The hotel room was smaller than the others had been, and its windows faced out on to the main road. Through the glass, red neon signs that promised pizza, kebabs and amusements swam against the night, bloody and blurred through a thin mist of rain.

'You didn't use the phone downstairs,' Rosina said, as he took off his jacket. 'Are you going to call from here?'

'No,' he said.

She leaned back against the wall and watched him. 'What

about Julia?'

It was somehow extraordinary to hear her speak the name. He had the sudden sense that time and worry had ceased to exist. 'I don't want to think about Julia. I'm with you.'

'I'm flattered,' she said gravely, turning towards the window.

He sat down heavily on the bed and watched her profile silhouetted against the darkness. 'I never know when you're being honest.'

'I'm always honest,' she said, and laughed. 'I'm never honest.'

'I don't understand you.'

'Perhaps I don't want you to.' Suddenly, she was enigmatic and reflective. She kicked off her shoes, with a child's blank-eyed absorption. 'Did you ever think of that?'

'Maybe.' He watched her intently. They would make love tonight, and he knew it just as she did – but he also knew that she was letting him set the pace for some reason of her own, and he wanted to know more of her secrets as if her conversation was a kind of foreplay. 'You didn't finish what you were going to tell me last time.'

'About what?'

'About a girl. Called Christine.'

'Oh,' she said, smiling. 'Her.'

'What happened with her?'

Her mocking eyes held him hypnotised. 'I suppose I ruined her life,' she said, 'if that doesn't sound too melodramatic.'

She came over to the bed and sat down beside him. He rested his hand on her thigh. The only sounds came from beyond the window – the muffled traffic noise, tooting horns, the occasional squeal of brakes. When he spoke, the sound of a human voice seemed all wrong. 'Why?' he asked. 'How?'

'I probably exaggerated,' she said thoughtfully. 'Not her life. Just a bit of her life. But I definitely changed her.'

'Tell me about it,' he said. 'I want to know about it.'

'All right.' She sat smooth, pale and composed beside him, her hand brushing his. 'We were at school together. She arrived in the third year, when we were fourteen. She didn't really fit in.'

'Why not?'

'She came from a bad area. I think it was a council estate or something. I can't quite remember,' she said. 'It was supposed to be a big deal for her to be there. She'd passed exams to get in. She was quite clever. In some ways.'

'A scholarship?'

'Something like that.' She brushed off the details indifferently before carrying on. 'Her parents were insane with pride. Beside themselves. I met them once or twice. They were even more pathetic than she was.'

'I thought you liked her.'

'I don't think I ever really *liked* her. Even at first. She was like a puppy who followed me around everywhere. It was fun to have her there. Sometimes. But I never really *liked* her.'

'But you put up with her.'

'That makes it sound as if I was being kind.' Her forehead creased in the effort of recollection. 'But that wasn't how it was at all. I suppose it was just about . . . power. She always did everything I said. I liked *that*.'

'What did you tell her to do?'

'Whatever I wanted.' She laughed. 'Nothing spectacular, really. I made her drink vodka and smoke a spliff once. In my room. It was so funny. She burst out crying and said she'd give anything to be me. Rambled on about her parents arguing all the time. Then passed out.' There was a long silence before she spoke again, her words edged with unmistakable contempt. 'She was absolutely *pathetic*. Like a little girl.'

Terry's mind stirred with images, disturbed by an indescribable darkness – Rosina smiling her small and secret smile in a Chelsea bedroom while her friend sobbed drunkenly, and the night pressing in outside just as it did now. 'So what did you do?' he asked slowly. 'To ruin her life?'

Rosina laughed again. 'I got her expelled.'

'Why?'

'Oh, not on purpose. I told you I quite liked having her

there. I did. But there was a teacher I hated. I wanted to get back at her for keeping me in detention after school so often. So I got Christine to do it with me.'

'What did you do?'

She ignored him. 'The teacher was called Mrs Martin. She was off on maternity leave for a while. Came back one day with her new arrival in a pram. Not to work. Just to show everyone. I made Christine offer to mind the baby for a minute while Mrs Martin went to the loo. Mrs Martin said yes. She liked Christine – at least, she did *then*. Thought she was such a sweet girl.'

He was aware of every breath he took. 'And?'

'We stole it,' she said, matter-of-factly. 'Wheeled it out of the school building and out of the grounds. By a side-route so nobody saw us, of course. We were going really fast. At first, the baby was laughing. Then it started screaming. It was a horrible little thing. I'd wanted to leave it in the ladies' toilets nearby, but it was making such a noise that people were staring at us. So we left it outside a newsagent.'

'*Rosina.*' He told himself that he was appalled, and that his sharp intake of breath had held no element of excitement. 'Anything could have happened to the baby, there.'

'That's what they said later. Who cares?' She brushed aside his interruption with a wave of her hand, and continued, 'Christine wanted us to tell someone where we'd left it. I told her I'd get her if she did. She believed me. I think she was quite scared of me by then. I told her to tell Mrs Martin she'd left it alone while she went to the tuck shop with me, and when she came back, it was gone.'

'She'd have been in trouble, just for that.'

'Oh, of course. But she probably wouldn't have been *expelled* for it. If she'd only had the sense to stick to the story,' she said. 'Of course, she didn't. I should have known. She just didn't have the guts.'

'What happened?'

'When we got back, everyone was frantic. I think Mrs Martin knew I'd had something to do with it. She and the head took Christine into a room and asked her questions. Apparently, she cracked almost at once. Burst into tears and told them everything.' For a second, her eyes were full of an absolute and hating fury. 'She couldn't do anything properly. She was just *pathetic*.'

'And?'

'Oh, someone had found the baby and called the police. Not that it was any help to me. I don't think Christine mentioned my name – don't think she'd have dared, even then. But we'd been seen together, pushing the pram. Some silly little bitch in the first year told on us. So we both got expelled.'

'What happened then?'

'Nothing much. My parents took it in their stride and found me another school. I don't think they really cared.' Again, he wondered at the lack of bitterness in her voice – it was as if she was talking about someone else, with chilly inhuman objectivity. '*Her* parents went mad. I heard them with her. How could you throw away this great chance and all the rest of it. Her mother was crying in the head's study – can you imagine that? No wonder Christine was so pathetic. She must have got it from them.'

'And then?' he asked, fascinated. 'What then?'

'Nothing, really. We didn't stay in touch. I couldn't be bothered with her any more. There was no point,' she said. 'She wrote to me eight or nine times. And phoned constantly. I just put the phone down. I think she got the message. Anyway, I haven't spoken to her in years.'

'So you don't know what she's doing now?'

'Who cares?' She turned and looked at him closely. Her hand brushed his wrist. 'Do you think I've told you enough now?'

'You'll never tell me enough,' he murmured, and then they were kissing and his hands were in her hair, and her textures were everything he'd ever dreamed they'd be and more.

White skin like raw silk. The brutality of need combined with impersonal tenderness beyond expression. Outside, an ambulance howled like a cat in the night. She threw back her head and screamed.

16

It was more than it had ever been with Marie, or the handful of girls who'd come before her. It was more than anything had ever been in his life. She became a part of the darkness that wound itself around him, her movements melting with his in an exquisite sensuality that was almost beyond endurance. She was cold, and she was anything but cold, and in the most intimate embrace of all, she seemed more distant and intriguing than she ever had before.

To think that he'd denied himself this for Marie's sake – he had a sudden image of her in the pub with her friends, thinking about Cheryl and Martin and Allie and Lisa and anything but him. The memory of her indifference vindicated him, relieved him of guilt. He felt that, in some way, he was repaying her for not caring.

Why did you say your sister was called Lisa, Terry?

No room for the voice here. No room for anxiety. No room for anything but immediate physical sensation and the here and now, and pleasure as instinctive as an animal's. Far away in his mind, pictures of Rodge and Sacker and Julia Fielding fell away as release approached, and when it came, his mother's image shattered into nothing.

He lay in the tangled sheets and stroked her, and she rose to meet his hands with arching feline movements, still smiling, always smiling. 'You like it,' she murmured, 'don't you?'

'Of course I do.' He found something soothing in her non-specific malice, away from the only world he knew – a million miles from the terrible dream. He felt safe with her, as he never felt safe now with Marie. 'You know I do,' and then she was in his arms again, and her raw-silk skin caressed him as they made love a second time.

When it was over and she was lying in his arms, sleep drifted in as easily as it never did in the talcum-scented bedroom. At one point, he thought they were kissing and his hands were in her hair, then something told him this was a dream – a little girl lay dead in a sunny orchard and the marks on her neck were livid – and apprehension mingled with his disappointment. A woman's voice entered the world, as the walls fell away, murmuring words that meant nothing in the dream – 'Goodbye,' it said quietly, 'goodnight.' When his eyes opened, his watch said it was half past five in the morning, and he was alone in a room not his own. There was no sign of Rosina, no note from Rosina. She'd gone.

17

His first thought was to call Marie from the phone by the bed. Then something stopped him, he wasn't sure what. Perhaps he was afraid that her anger might bring him back too sharply to reality, but it was more than that. A small, frightened, childish part of him *wanted* her to worry, not for revenge but just to prove that she cared – her relief in the kitchen when he got home after work telling him she wasn't really indifferent, her arms closing around him when he stepped inside, sweet as a reprieve. All he knew was, he couldn't bring himself to ring her at home. Not now.

You said your sister's name was Lisa, last night in the club, the little voice reminded him. *Why did you say that, Terry?*

But he didn't have an answer to that, and he got out of bed quickly and suddenly, as if to escape it.

In the stark little bathroom, he thought he could smell Rosina's perfume – it mocked him, with cold blue eyes that missed nothing, as he stepped under the shower and washed himself. It occurred to him that he'd brought no razor, shaving-foam or toothbrush with him, and that he'd have to get hold of some before he went into work. Under thin needles of lukewarm water, he felt the hated office waiting for him, and Rosina's magic was gone.

He put on the clothes he'd worn the previous day, and went back into the bedroom. Suddenly, it looked ugly, anonymous: the quality of the darkness had changed to become bleak and sordid – tangled sheets had nothing to do with last night's rapture. Although it wasn't yet six o'clock, there was no point in lingering here. He put on his coat, walked out onto the landing and down the stairs to the foyer, aware of his dishevelled appearance.

Behind the reception desk, a large middle-aged woman with bare arms as thick as thighs took his key and hung it on a row of hooks behind her. 'Come back again some time, sir,' she called. 'Have a nice day.' Terry smiled at her then left, his mind swarming with a hundred uncertainties.

The early morning was icy, raw and shadowed. It had stopped raining at some point in the small hours, and streetlights reflected off the dark wet pavement. When Terry glanced back at the hotel it looked different – he might never have seen it before – and he felt disoriented. Suddenly it seemed possible that last night had been nothing but a vivid dream – that there was no hostess bar named Delilah's in Soho, no black-haired girl called Rosina who fascinated him like a riddle.

Is Marie worried about you, Terry? Will she be pleased to see you again? Or are you just imagining that, too?

He flinched away from the voice and hurried on, following the signs to Victoria station. In its echoing, near-deserted concourse, the shops had just started to open. He bought toothbrush, toothpaste, shaving-foam and razors in Boots, then brushed his teeth and shaved in the station Gents. A pale strange face watched him tensely from the mirrors. 'Rosina,' he murmured. The name seemed to echo in the wilderness of polished chrome and porcelain before it was swept away by more immediate terrors: Sacker and Rob and Christian, the appalling dream, the prospect of approaching redundancy.

And Marie.

More than anything, Marie.

18

'Hello?'

'Hi, Allie.' Marie sat at her desk with the receiver pressed to her ear. Her hand had clenched around it so tightly that her knuckles were white. 'It's me.'

'Marie? What's wrong?'

'It's Terry. He didn't come home last night.'

'My God,' said Allie. 'Didn't he phone or anything?'

'No. I haven't heard a word.'

The door to Marie's office was closed, but she still spoke quietly. She couldn't bear to be overheard, didn't want even Sandra to know about it. Other people's vicarious worry would only increase hers.

'Where are you calling from?' asked Allie. 'Home?'

'Work.'

'I can't believe you went into the office today, Marie! Couldn't you have called in and explained?'

'What's the point? Just so I could sit on my own at home, worrying myself sick all day?' Her voice wobbled – she steadied it with an effort. 'I thought it'd take my mind off things a bit. Coming in as usual. Having things to do.'

'Well . . . if it makes you feel better . . .' There was a brief, tense silence before Allie spoke again. 'Have you tried his work number?'

'I haven't *got* his work number.' The random pettiness of this made her want to cry – she blinked back tears with a great effort. 'He moved offices a few weeks ago. I kept reminding myself to get it from him and write it down somewhere but . . .' and she lapsed into a beaten, frightened silence.

'Well, have you called the police?'

'Yeah. First thing this morning, when I woke up and he wasn't there,' said Marie. 'They said there wasn't anything they could do. He has to be gone twenty-four hours before they report him as missing.'

'God,' said Allie quietly. 'I don't know what to say.'

'Neither do I.' There was no point in talking any more – there was nothing left to say, she'd told her sister all she knew. 'Well, I'll let you know, Allie, as soon as I hear anything.'

'Okay,' said Allie uncertainly, ''bye.'

Now she wasn't talking any more, Marie found the near-silence almost unearthly – voices filtering occasionally through her office door provided the only sounds in the world. A terrible new suspicion surfaced. Terry's mental-breakdown mood, his solitary hours in the study, the times she couldn't tell what he was thinking . . . The more she thought about it, the more plausible the idea became. He'd been thinking about suicide for the last few weeks, had found some way of killing himself away from home.

If he was all right, he would have called her long before now. He must know that she'd be worried to death, that she'd be distracted all day at work. He wouldn't do that to her, she thought, even now. A sudden image came to her of Terry collapsed in a gents' cubicle where the walls reached down to the floor, having taken an overdose of something she'd not known he had. Terry, pale and dead somewhere in this city, slumped against a wall, his body waiting to be discovered . . .

19

'You heard yet?' asked Christian. 'They've chucked out Martin Harris.'

'When's the party?' asked Alex.

'Come on,' said Rob. 'He wasn't as bad as some of the suits.'

'Fucking wanker, more like,' said Alex. 'You know what he

did to me and Lucy's Vodafone campaign? He didn't even show it to the client, the spineless little fuck.'

'Yeah,' said Lucy. 'We should go out and celebrate after work. One less useless account handler for us to worry about . . .'

Terry sat at his desk, his skull throbbing. The wave had arrived at last, and would sweep him away in a matter of weeks. Him and Rodge. Across the desk, Rodge seemed intent on his computer screen, but Terry knew he was straining to catch every word. 'Reckon Nigel Cartman's on his way out, and all,' Christian was saying. 'Heard from Gavin that he—'

Terry couldn't bear to listen to any more. He got up and went to the kitchen. As he waited for the kettle to boil, his eyes strayed over to the notice board, where Rob, Christian, Alex and Lucy grinned out at him from a photograph taken at the awards do last Friday night. The boys were in tuxedos, Lucy in off-the-shoulder black. Rob and Christian held their statuette aloft between them, obviously drunk, agonisingly triumphant. The happiness in that photograph tore at him deep inside.

That was you, once, the little voice reminded him, with a smirk. *And by the way, Terry, are you sure Marie's going to be pleased to see you tonight? Are you sure she's not really hoping you've gone for good?*

At half past twelve, he left the office, and walked to NatWest, where he queued at the cashpoint for some time. He got out the card that Marie didn't know about, put it into the machine and pressed Balance Enquiry. The five-figure sum stared out at him. The sight of it stirred possibilities in his mind – but he couldn't put a name to them. He got back his card and hurried to the office, stopping off at Pret A Manger to buy lunch.

What are you really thinking of, Terry? Marie – or something else?

In the afternoon, he and Rodge sat in one of the little meeting rooms, coming up with ideas for a one-off travel brochure. The silence was intensely claustrophobic. Any tiny point of contact he'd ever had with Rodge had vanished: terror had driven them into separate isolation booths. They were marked men, and knew it. 'What about "Sun and Fun"?' Rodge asked at last, in a voice that had nothing in common with his normal strident delivery, and Terry knew that Rodge knew the idea was useless, but he smiled and nodded anyway. And as he wrote down the words on his pad, a sense of inevitability touched him: there was no point in even *trying* now, and the single sentence on the lined A4 said it all. They sat in silence, and were condemned.

Minutes ticked out slowly on his watch as the darkness pressed in beyond the window. A few more spastic ideas were born, maintained their tenuous grip on life, were mechanically transcribed on paper. 'Well,' said Rodge at last, 'suppose it's time to call it a day.' As they gathered their belongings and returned to the office, Terry's feeling of finality blossomed into nightmare – his last hour of grace was fading around him, leaving only Marie.

What's she going to say when you get in, Terry? Is she going to hug you, or—?

Terry turned his computer off and put on his coat. 'Well,' he said to nobody in particular, 'see you tomorrow.' But Rodge was hanging round the lads on the table football, and nobody watched him leave.

20

When Marie got home she checked the answerphone for messages. None had been left. There was a leaden feeling in the pit of her stomach. Throughout the slow hours of her afternoon at work, her image of Terry lying dead in a toilet cubicle had become too vivid to be anything but the truth. The only remaining question in her mind was who would call to tell her, and when.

She sat down in the kitchen but, as the minutes ticked away, inactivity became impossible. Something drove her to her feet and out of the room. She didn't know where she was going until she was at the study door, pushing it open, heading for the desk and switching on the light.

What are you doing? a little voice demanded querulously. *And why?* But she knew the answer to both questions perfectly well. It didn't feel as if there was anything to lose now. And she needed to know the truth.

Discover her husband's secrets.

She sat down at the desk in the pale compass-circle of lamplight and started opening the drawers. The first and second were virtually empty. The third held a blank pad of A4 and a hole-punch. *There's nothing here*, she told herself. *He's hidden it all away somewhere else.* But another part of her knew differently. She opened the last drawer and froze.

It was a photograph album, old but far from dilapidated, bound in ox-blood leather, the size of a coffee-table book. She took it out, set it down on the desk in front of her, and opened it.

The first page showed a glossy, studio-quality photograph of a little girl she'd never seen before. She didn't look as if she had anything to do with Terry, Marie thought. There was no link to her husband in this sweet, stocky, round-faced child with the bright golden hair and rosy cheeks. Pale Terry with his hair that was almost white, his iced-water eyes. The child wore a pretty flowered dress, and her hair fell in ringlets round her face. Marie could almost see the professional photographer murmuring encouragements behind the mounted tripod, the loving parents smiling indulgently behind him.

But what the hell's this got to do with Terry? she thought urgently, and turned the page.

Six more photographs, three on each side. All neatly mounted behind clear plastic, and all of the same little girl. A younger version, identifable by the sweet rosy face and golden curls, laughing in a foamy bathtub; hugging a glossily wrapped present in front of a Christmas tree; holding a vast doll in the same setting, smiling into the camera. It was a captivating smile – a smile of innocence, confidence, unselfconscious trust in the world.

She turned the pages. The little girl in summer dresses and in winter coats, the little girl in dungarees, and shorts, and a frothy, elaborate party dress of cream-coloured lace. Behind her, nothing that specified any recognisable time or place – a vague hint of solid respectable prosperity in dark gleaming wood and well-tended greenery, a series of photographs as perfect as an ad campaign. Who took this many photographs of a child? Marie wondered. What kind of adoring parents needed a record so comprehensive?

Another page was turned. Another. Another. And everywhere Marie looked, she was met by the same captivating smile, the same sense of love behind the camera, unseen for ever.

Marie turned the page again.

No photographs here. The left-hand page was blank. The right-hand one showed the front page of a newspaper, yellowed with age. The date in the top corner was 10 July 1975. The headline screamed VICAR'S DAUGHTER MURDERED IN GARDEN alongside the first photograph she'd seen in the album.

It's his sister, Marie thought starkly. *The one he's never really talked about, who died when she was six, who he's never even shown me a picture of.* Horror engulfed her. Her heart was hammering so hard that she didn't hear the front door open, or the footsteps in the hallway. It was only the sharp intake of breath behind her that made her whirl round in her seat.

Terry was standing in the study doorway.

21

For an endless second, the spike-point of her horror trembled where it was, then collapsed around something even more immediate. He wasn't dead and he wasn't injured and he *hadn't even phoned.* Her bewilderment fuelled her fear – which intensified her rage.

'That's *mine,*' he said, in a slow, stunned voice. 'You *can't* look at that. It's *private.*'

She sat where she was and stared back at him. When she spoke, she didn't recognise the furious voice that emerged. 'Never mind what I'm looking at! Where the *fuck* have you been?'

He might as well not have heard her. 'I told you that's mine! Give it to me!'

A few steps forward and he grabbed it, wrenching it out of her hands – he snatched it away, and almost *leaped* back. Bizarrely, he held the album behind his back as if to hide it from her, although she'd seen all there was to see. While she had every reason to be terrified, she felt suddenly anaesthetised. There was no such thing as fear in the world: there was only red pulsating anger.

'For Christ's sake, what the hell is the matter with you? You're acting like you're going mad or something! Where were you all last night?'

Still he held the album behind his back. His eyes flickered with a child's apprehension that was worse than his moment of violence – something stunted, helpless, grotesque in a man's body. 'We were working on a new account till gone midnight. I stopped over at a hotel in town. I would have called, but I didn't want to wake you—'

'Didn't want to *wake* me? Do you know I almost missed work today because of you? I thought you were dead, I thought you were *fucking dead* and *you didn't want to wake me*?' She broke off for a second. 'So what about today? Why didn't you call me at work?'

His shoulders rose and fell, and he looked at the floor with the photograph album held behind him. She hadn't known that her anger could increase, but it did. 'Don't just *shrug* like that!' she exploded. 'What the hell's the matter with you?' Still he stood, wordless, and his silence incensed her. 'Sitting up all night looking at that book of yours. Like something out of the fucking *Shining*. What did you think you were playing at last night? *Why didn't you call me?*'

His voice was so quiet that it was almost inaudible. 'I really thought you'd care.'

'Oh, I care.' An image of Robert flashed behind Marie's eyes – she was in the grip of an anger beyond the world. 'I care that you sit in here like a zombie every night – I care that you couldn't even be bothered to *call*. Why didn't you? *Why didn't you?*'

He looked at her directly. Something in his eyes replaced her huge anger with an equally huge fear. It was like coming face to face with a distilled essence of hatred. There was no sanity in that look. None at all.

'*I thought you'd care about me*,' he ground out, and then he turned. A few seconds passed before the front door slammed behind him with shuddering force.

She hadn't used his name. Not once.

Julia, he'd said in the club last week, and he could hear his own voice as clearly as a sound recording, underscored by drifting music and the clink of glass on glass from another table. *Julia Fielding*.

He walked through a night as dark and infinite as outer space and became aware that he still had the album in his hand, the photographic record of Katie's life and Katie's murder that his mother had compiled long ago, that he'd found and kept after her death. It had never occurred to him that Marie might seek it out; he wondered how much she'd seen. Suddenly he felt a bone-deep conviction that there was no safe place to keep it now, that he'd have to get rid of it.

It didn't matter. He didn't need the photographs to remind him of what he was capable. He had had the voice to do that recently – the voice and the dream. Passing a street bin, he threw in the ox-blood-leather album without a second thought. It had been all-important to him once and now it meant nothing.

Like so much else . . .

I care that you couldn't even be bothered to call, he remembered, and then the insidious little voice took over from Marie's, deep in his head, gloating over his anguish with superficial saccharine sympathy. *Oh, yes, Terry. She cares all right. Only not about you any more . . .*

Bright pub lights glowed across the road, and he crossed to meet them – he couldn't stand to walk any longer in this icy darkness, he needed warmth and light and noise. Inside, the pub was shabby, smoky and crowded. He bought a double whisky at the bar and sat alone at a table by the window, noise from the pool table and the jukebox running through his head as he looked out into the night. Car headlights moved behind his reflected image. A black-haired girl name Rosina was out there somewhere, and the knowledge had become all he had left to believe in – in her malicious, inscrutable way, she seemed to embody a kind of salvation.

And you need salvation now, Terry. You really need salvation . . .

When he'd finished his drink, he got another, and another. Alcoholic oblivion had become his only escape from the voice that tormented him. But while he could evade the voice, there was no hiding from the memories – the more he drank, the more his thoughts blurred around the image of Katie lying dead in the orchard, and how he'd felt running back to the house, and how the sun had blazed down as he'd approached the back door and seen his mother cooking in the kitchen.

You've got to come quickly. It's Katie—

Julia Fielding whirling round, her face draining. A bitter and terrible satisfaction at the sight of her fear. He could move her in some way, at least. At last—

I think Katie's dead—

The bell behind the bar rang for last orders. He bought another double whisky, took it back to his table, and sat looking out at the bleak, lonely night. He thought about Katie until the barman called that it was closing time, and the harsh overhead lights went on, and there was nowhere left for him to go but home. Outside, the cold air hit him hard, and Katie's face stayed in his mind throughout the endless walk back.

When home came in sight, he saw that all the lights were off. He let himself in quietly, closed and bolted the front door behind him, ascended the stairs that were faintly lit by moonlight. The bedroom door was closed. He knew that Marie was lying sleepless and alert behind it, ready to scream at him to get out the second the doorhandle turned. It hurt him – and more. It enraged him.

I care that you couldn't even be bothered to call, she had spat, and he went into the bathroom, splashed his face with water that was colder and fresher than any he'd felt before. It did nothing to calm him. He felt the effects of the double whiskies as an intensification of his hatred for her. For her and little Katie.

Lisa. Her name's Lisa, Terry.

Suddenly, even the voice had no power. There was no room for anything but a raw, murderous fury for the people who didn't care about him. He went into the spare room and lay down on the bed, fully clothed. He lay with his eyes closed for a long time before a kind of peace overcame him, and he slept.

22

He woke slowly. Something in the quality of the light was wrong, and he understood at once that he'd overslept. He checked his watch, and saw it had just gone nine thirty. He'd slept until gone nine thirty and Marie hadn't woken him.

He got out of bed and realised that he'd fallen asleep in the same clothes he'd been wearing for the last two days. He must look like a tramp, he thought, but it didn't matter. He had more important things to do this morning than change his clothes, because he'd faded out completely, and there was only one thing left for him.

A new sense of serenity. Emptiness and silence echoed in his head. Beyond the window, the sky was a deep indigo, the shade of a gnarled plum. He observed it without surprise. This was an apocalyptic morning, and it seemed only fitting that the weather should reflect that.

He padded downstairs, hearing a murmur of voices from the kitchen. He recognised them as Marie and Lisa's. He experienced a moment's surprise – they hadn't been expecting Lisa that day and Marie should be at work by now – but then he realised that it didn't matter: it was right that the two of them should be here this morning, wasn't it? More than right. The only way . . .

He walked into the kitchen. Marie and Lisa sat at the table, Lisa picking at a bowl of cornflakes, Marie watching her affectionately. Neither looked round as he came in, or registered his presence in any way. It was as if he was invisible.

'You've got to keep your strength up, Lisa,' Marie was saying. 'We're going to the cinema later, and . . .'

He let her words die around him. They didn't matter, because nothing mattered any more, and he was conscious of nothing but an overwhelming tranquillity. He had found peace at last, and he moved unobserved towards the cutlery drawer, and took out the sharp butcher's knife that Marie always used for carving roasts, and unsheathed it from its protective plastic. And he came up behind Lisa and plunged the blade deep into the back of her neck.

Blood sprayed up in a scarlet fountain, and Marie saw him in the same instant that she saw Lisa's death. Her hand flew to her mouth and she screamed. He pulled the blade free with an unspeakable gristly noise that didn't seem important, and turned the knife on her. Again and again he stabbed her, again and again and again. A remote, inhuman joy combined with his new peace as the blood flew, and the freedom of a gnarled plum sky filled the world.

23

Rosina lay awake. She'd got back from the club an hour ago and couldn't sleep. Terry hadn't been in that night, and – while he'd stayed away much longer in the past – his single absence had made her distrust his motives.

It was crazy. She knew he didn't just want her for sex, that he wouldn't walk away now he'd had it. But a small, cynical part of her couldn't help doubting. She kept thinking of a married man hurrying back to his wife after a night of passion in a cheap hotel, a tacky little cliché like the basis for a dirty joke. It disturbed her. Surely the night they'd spent together had meant more than *that.*

But perhaps that *was* all it had meant to him. The more she thought about it, the stronger her suspicion became that he'd be just as drawn to Vicki, or Roxanne, or any of the girls at the club, that all he wanted was sex and the thrill of having a secret, that deep inside he looked at her and saw anyone at all.

She envisaged a bored, unfaithful married man climbing into bed beside a dull wife, and making up some plausible excuse as to where he'd been all night, and kissing her goodnight before falling asleep – a man over whom Rosina had no genuine power whatsoever. And it had been important to their relationship that she had power over him. It had been essential—

It's only a joke, Chris. Stop being so pathetic.

But it's wrong, Rosina. I don't want to do it. Besides, we'll get in trouble.

Who cares? Do you want to carry on being my friend?

Of course I do. You know I do, but—

There had been power then, Rosina remembered. Near-absolute. She could recall every last detail of that time: Mrs Martin's voice in the hallway before she turned away, the brief murmured exchange after the toilet door closed behind her. How it had felt hurrying down the corridor with the pram. The baby laughing.

But, Rosina—

Shut up. We're not out of the grounds, yet.

But, Rosina—

I said, shut up*!*

The fresh green smell of summer and cut grass, the occasional cars that passed them along the road; their occupants would see a dark girl and a blonde girl walking with a pram, the blonde girl terrified, the dark girl simmering with laughter that wasn't even human enough to be cruel. A strange ambiguous amusement that could snap into fury in the blink of an eye. The baby crying.

We can't leave him here!

We can. We are.

But, Rosina – Rosina—

Christine Molloy, the baby-faced blonde she'd come to hate beyond words – the definitive helpless victim. The memory of her pleading voice brought Rosina sharply back into the present, and the charcoal shadows of a room that always smelt of Escape. She'd thought Terry shared stupid little Christine's masochistic fascination, but maybe he didn't after all. At the end of the day, he'd gone back to his wife, and she was alone here.

When he next comes into the club, she thought, I'll look

him in the eye and find out what he really feels, and she lay back on the pillow, trying too hard not to think that he might never come back. She had to be everything to him, because that was how she'd planned it from the start – because she was Rosina, and her plans always paid off.

24

Terry's eyes opened to silence and darkness in the spare bedroom. His heart was pounding harder and faster than he'd ever known it to. His forehead was cold and slick with sweat.

The dream. The terrible dream.

It always came fresh to him, no matter how often he had it. It always came fresh and it always seemed real, always blended into reality so that it became indistinguishable from life. He'd woken in the spare room fully clothed, and he'd been supposed to go into work, because it had been Wednesday morning in the dream and it was Wednesday morning today. Then he'd gone down into the kitchen, and he'd—

No. NO.

Oh, yes, Terry. Yes. And by the way, Terry, how do you think it's going to feel when you don't wake up afterwards? When the darkness comes down like it did all those years ago, and when it lifts, you're standing in the kitchen with their blood on the walls . . .

An iron fist gripped down on his guts – he was seized by a terror beyond expression. Because the dream wasn't that far-fetched. He was a conscientious employee, and he'd tried his best over the years to be a good husband, but he'd been a well-behaved little boy twenty-seven years ago, and when it had come to the crunch, it hadn't mattered at all. When he'd been ten years old, he'd still killed his sister, and he was beginning to feel closer and closer to killing his wife and niece.

Book Three

1

He hadn't hated Katie. Not at first.

'You've got a little sister, Terry,' his father had said to him jovially. He'd only been four, but he could still remember the sentence word for word. It was rare for either of his parents to speak to him like that, to sound affectionate or indulgent, even at a time of celebration. Julia Fielding was never so happy that she used that tone with him. Even right after the birth of her daughter.

To begin with, Terry had greeted his sister's arrival with cautious hope. He had a vague idea that he might not have to be alone any more, now that he had Katie. Maybe, when she got older, she'd feel the same as he did now, and they could share secrets and fears, and keep each other company.

But by the time she was two, he had known that his dreams weren't going to come true. She had nothing in common with him, and never would. She was carefree. She was happy. She was loved.

To begin with, he admired her for that, even though the admiration grew a little more tinged with envy every year. Not jealousy, but the wistful longing of comparing himself to a creature of another species. How easily she laughed, chattered, hugged – how unafraid she was of anything. Perhaps that was why their mother loved her so much more, why she led their father to do the same. Perhaps it was just that Katie *deserved* to be loved better.

But by the time he was eight, he'd changed his mind about that – and, as a direct corollary, about Katie. He had started to think that she was only the way she was because she was loved and cherished, that it wasn't a cause, but a result. The knowledge cast unfairness over everything like a too-bright light. It was easy to be confident and winsome when people cared about you. He would have laughed and chattered just as endearingly, if they'd ever cared about *him.*

Distant anger began to stir in him. Sometimes, he had strange, dark dreams of violence but, temporarily disturbing as they were, they didn't seem important. Not then.

By the time he was nine, the dreams had got worse, and more frequent. He didn't know why – nothing had *changed* about his life, but it had stopped being merely unpleasant and become almost unbearable. He hated the isolation of the playground and the classroom, and there was never any comfort in going home. Perhaps because he wasn't quite a child any more, he could see things more clearly, and his sense of unfairness turned into something like a constant migraine.

His mother wasn't a queen or a goddess, as he'd always perceived her in the past; she wasn't guided in her indifference by some omniscient wisdom. She was a cold, uncaring, neurotic woman who had taken a dislike to her son for some petty reason of her own. Did she harbour a deep dislike for the opposite sex? Might her preference for Katie be as simple as that? Quite possibly. She even treated her own husband with thinly veiled contempt, for all that he adored her. But at the end of the day none of this mattered to her nine-year-old son. All that mattered was that she was fallible, and that she was in the wrong.

His father wasn't a wise god, either. For the first time, Terry perceived Paul Fielding as he really was: a big, unimaginative, stolid and rather foolish man, with no thoughts in his head that hadn't been implanted by either the Bible or Julia Fielding. He was absolutely under his wife's thumb, and watched her walk in and out of rooms with a dog's adoration. Nothing for Terry to admire there, either. Nothing sacrosanct.

And then there was Katie. Always there was Katie, reminding him of everything he'd been denied. Contentment. Fearlessness. Optimism.

The nightmares grew worse. He began to dream about killing her.

2

That old Harkness, the hard lads said. *Reckon he's a pervert.*

Terry didn't know why it seemed to matter, or why it stuck in his mind. Recently it had been difficult to think clearly about the things that mattered. Almost every night was crowded with the dream, and his days were crowded with evasions and denials of it.

Always the same dream. She was in the orchard, playing there as she often did. He walked up to her with a length of rope hidden behind his back. He smiled. She smiled.

Do you want to play a game, Katie? he asked. *It's a good game. I'll show you how to play it.*

She looked at him quizzically with bright blue eyes.

Turn round, he said. *Close your eyes.*

She did. He came up behind her. Strangling her with the rope was easy and it was then that he always woke up. At the moment when her muscles went limp and she collapsed. No matter how often he had that dream, it never lost any of its power, any of its impact.

How vivid her death became in the darkness of his room, how longed-for. The force of his own longing frightened him. His mind started to skip, to play tricks on him. Some days, he couldn't remember getting up, had no recollection of the walk to school. He must have come downstairs, for he was sitting in the kitchen eating breakfast, but the vague memory of washing his face and brushing his teeth could have come from yesterday, or the day before, or some time next year. Moments of blackness, like a curtain falling in his head – solid hours in which he moved and spoke on autopilot, and couldn't remember doing anything at all.

Was that preoccupation? What that fear – or insanity?

Worse, the inner workings of his mind were becoming just as alien to him as his movements. As he had no idea how he'd come into school some mornings, he had no idea why he'd told his mother about old Harkness looking at Katie, or why he'd told the few boys with whom he was friendly the same thing. It was uncharacteristic of him to confide in people. After the hometime bell had rung recently, he'd started going for long walks on his own, down narrow semi-rural lanes dappled with the shadows of overhead leaves. He couldn't have said what he thought about at those times. Part of him believed he thought about nothing.

But a hidden part of him, the part that brought the dreams, must have known differently, because when he'd been ten for almost three weeks, his mind took the greatest skip of all. The curtain came down when he was walking past his mother, out of the vicarage kitchen, a solid black curtain behind his eyes that cut off the world. When it lifted again – seemingly a split second later – he was standing in the orchard, looking down at his sister's lifeless body. She was lying up against the trunk of an apple tree, and the marks on her neck were livid. The skipping rope lay in the grass beside her, abandoned, coiled like a snake.

Cartoonish bees hovered round the wildflowers. From far away in the distance came the murmured hint of a cricket match. Terry heard none of it. He looked down at his sister's body with disbelief. This was reality. And, while he had no memory of the events, he'd killed her, just as he'd dreamed so many times of doing . . .

They'll know, he thought, but they didn't.

Robert Harkness was arrested almost at once.

3

Terry didn't mention Harkness's name. People had thought of it on their own. Harkness had no alibi, nobody who'd seen him leading his solitary life away from the Fielding orchard that afternoon. He said he'd been alone in his flat. It didn't matter. Nobody believed him.

Terry hadn't understood why he'd told his mother and his peers about old Harkness looking at Katie – he'd thought perhaps it had been out of concern. But, of course, that was ridiculous. How could he have been concerned about a sister he'd dreamed of killing – who'd been murdered in the exact way he'd imagined?

He found it more frightening than anything, even worse than the overwhelming guilt, to think that he'd set up an innocent man without realising he was doing it. That he'd been planning, and hadn't been aware that he'd been planning at all.

The blackouts came to an abrupt end. It was as if the act of murder had flipped a switch to turn them off, leaving him with nothing inside but a cold, terrible lucidity.

His mother's expression when Harkness's name was mentioned – Terry knew then and there that he'd never forget it. Her lips compressed in a bloodless line, glacial hatred behind the pain in her eyes, vengeance in every line of her face. How narrowly he'd escaped, Terry thought – how easily that look could have been for him.

And he wondered what he'd said to his sister before he'd tightened the rope round her neck, and how exactly he'd done it, and whether she'd had time to scream. But however frantically he combed his memory, there was nothing but solid black, and he began to understand that he'd never know.

The case made headlines. The press referred to it as *the vicarage murder.* The phone rang incessantly, and Julia Fielding wrenched the cord out of its socket. Robert Harkness was crucified on a dozen front pages, was sentenced to life imprisonment at the trial, killed himself in a cell three days later. It seemed a fitting dénouement, and after that the press lost interest.

When Terry heard of Harkness's suicide he found himself in the grip of crushing, devastating guilt that led him to the brink of confession three times in quick succession. He had new nightmares, in which Harkness smiled out from under his bed and Katie walked into the kitchen with livid marks on her neck to tell their parents what he'd done. He didn't sleep for days. One morning, terror and exhaustion led him to collapse in the classroom, and a kind teacher called in Paul and Julia Fielding, and he thought that the three of them looked at him oddly. It was then that self-preservation kicked in, and it spoke in a rational little voice that he'd never heard before in his life: *They think you're grieving for Katie, Terry. But it's going to look odd if you don't stop grieving soon. Maybe people might start putting two and two together. It's not likely. But it's not impossible.*

But I can't stop, he replied urgently in his mind. *How am I supposed to stop thinking about it?*

Just remind yourself that you're safe now. The little voice was adult, implacable. *You'll never do anything like that again. You'll never even do anything wrong again. You'll pass your O levels and A levels, and you'll go to university and you'll get a good job and you'll get married. And the nightmares – they'll fade in time, Terry. Maybe not disappear, but they'll fade. By the time you're thirty, you'll have maybe one a year.*

It brought him back to himself, that voice. He started sleeping better, stopped feeling as if he was about to confess or collapse at any second. He had never worked harder at school, or been more silently obedient at home. He'd been reprieved. The least he could do in return was study when his teachers told him to, and stay in his room when his parents didn't want him around.

In the slow years following Katie's death, life at the vicarage changed. Julia Fielding grew thinner and more preoccupied than ever: she was frightened and fragile in a way she'd never been before, although no more affectionate to her husband or her son. She took on a hollow-eyed look, and the doctor prescribed sleeping pills. When Terry was twelve, his father found her dead. She'd taken an overdose, whether deliberate or accidental, nobody knew. Terry thought it was probably deliberate. She'd never been the same since Katie's murder.

Three deaths on Terry's conscience, now . . . but he could feel no real guilt for the third.

The change in Paul Fielding was more subtle. At home and with his son, he was quiet and withdrawn – in church and with his parishioners, he was more jovial and outgoing than ever. It was an odd response to desolation, but not unique. Years later, Terry would be reminded of it by a colleague called Rodge.

Terry went to Exeter University, slaved for a higher second in English literature, and was snapped up by an up-and-coming advertising agency shortly after graduation. He was a talented copywriter with a great future ahead of him, and he met a pretty, bright-eyed brunette in a post-office queue. Her uncritical adoration touched him with something that felt like true love, and he married her six months later. She never asked what he was thinking, took the summary of his past at face value and seemed to see his father as the congregation did.

When he was twenty-nine, he won a major industry award at a ceremony held at the Dorchester, and came home with a bottle of champagne under his arm to share his joy with his wife. And the future looked glorious. They'd have a son together soon, he thought, and everything would be perfect, and Katie's ghostly image would fade into nothing.

But the future hadn't happened. What could have been a promising start instead became the beginning of the end. One failed pitch led to a failed campaign, which led to another, which led to a third. The third had cost him his job, and he joined a new agency with all of it counting against him from the outset, getting older all the time, with fresh ideas seeming more unreachable, and awards like a half-forgotten dream. Becoming the kind of uninspired, dutiful wordsmith he'd despised in his early career as inflation overtook his salary, a new generation drifted into the industry, and his colleagues slowly began to write him off. Leading up to the Monday-morning meetings in Soho Square, feeling the world crashing down around him all over again . . .

And the only way of averting murder now seemed to lie in escaping.

Escaping everything.

With Rosina.

4

Marie set the steaming cup of coffee by Terry's hand without speaking. This morning there didn't seem to be anything to say. Yesterday's terror seemed distant yet clear. She'd sat in the study looking through photographs of an unknown little girl and thinking her husband was dead. Then he'd come back, and—

He hasn't even said sorry. Not once, she thought, and told herself that was what niggled at her. She didn't want to come to terms with the strangeness of him looking at that photograph album every night, with the look he'd given her just before he had stormed out.

She sat down at the table across from him. It was up to him, she knew, to say something first, to apologise or at least explain, but he didn't. Just sat in an absolute silence that he didn't seem to notice, and sipped his coffee until it was gone.

'I have to go,' he said abruptly, not meeting her eyes. 'I'll be late for work.' He walked out of the kitchen, and she saw him put on his coat in the hallway. Then he left, and the front door swung shut behind him.

He'd slammed it last night. Suddenly, she couldn't dismiss that any more – the expression in his eyes and the way he'd held the photograph album behind his back, the dozens and dozens of pictures of a little girl with corn-coloured hair and rosy cheeks. It was a relief that he'd left for work, she thought – and was appalled by a new realisation: she didn't want to be around him any more, his presence upset her. For the first time, she had the sense that their marriage was intolerable.

It was only his sister, she told herself. *Of course he'd want to keep some record of her. He was only ten when she was killed.* But her internal voice lacked conviction. In all the years they'd been married, she'd heard him mention Katie perhaps four times – when there was no way to avoid the subject. It was bizarre to find that his apparent indifference concealed something like obsession – that he sat up in the small hours of the morning, looking at images of a child who'd never grown up . . .

But there was no point in tormenting herself with unwelcome thoughts. She was due in the office at nine. In front of the hallway mirror, she brushed her hair and wondered how she'd explain Terry's reappearance to Allie. She couldn't possibly tell her sister what he'd told her – she'd think it so weird. Just as she did, she mused, and saw that her treacherous train of thought had led her straight back to what she didn't want to face – a claustrophobic marriage, a husband who was growing stranger day by day.

Think about Robert, she urged herself. As she stepped out of the house into the cold morning, she clung to the attractive head of Strategy's image like a lifebelt. There were normal, unthreatening things out there, and he seemed to epitomise every one of them – easy, straightforward relationships, laughter in pleasant wine bars, a shared joke at work and warm, honest eyes. Marie turned up Streatham high street, full of an intense longing to go out with him again, knowing that if he asked her out a second time she'd accept at once.

5

'Nigel Cartman's got the chop,' said Rob, as he came back from the staff kitchen. 'Ran into Maria a minute ago. She said he just left the building in tears.'

'Fucking wuss. Good riddance,' said Alex, and laughed. 'Never liked him anyway.'

'How many account handlers have they got rid of now?' asked Lucy.

'Five, isn't it? Esther, Jez, Nigel, Martin, and that bitch from Gavin's team. You know, the one who reckoned she was Alexis Colby.'

'She knows where she can stick her shoulder-pads,' said Christian, and the laughter rolled again, and swept over to Terry's desk like an echo from another world. 'You reckon they're going to chuck any more of the suits out?'

'Maria says that's it for them,' said Rob. 'They're having a meeting tomorrow in the boardroom. Put their minds at rest, and all that shit.'

'When do you reckon they're going to start on us lot?' asked Alex idly. 'You reckon they'll leave it till Monday or—'

'Let's go and carry on with the holiday ideas, eh, Terry?'

Across the desk, Rodge's voice was too loud, and suddenly had nothing to do with confidence or comedy. Terry looked up, and saw that Rodge had got up from his seat, that he was gripping his sketch-pad so tightly that his knuckles were pale. The others had fallen silent at the sound of his voice, and were watching the two of them, making no effort to disguise their off-hand and speculative curiosity. 'Okay,' Terry said quietly. 'Let's go and find a spare room.' And as he walked out of the office with Rodge, he knew that Rob and Christian, Alex and Lucy would start talking about them as soon as they were out of earshot, and Alex would laugh, and Lucy wouldn't care, and Rob and Christian would sympathise in a rough, throwaway manner that was more damning than anything else.

He sat with Rodge in one of the little meeting rooms. Neither spoke for endless minutes. When Rodge finally did, it was with a new intensity that took Terry by surprise. 'I can't think of anything today,' he said.

Terry looked out of the window into the grey morning and the faceless people who moved six floors down. 'Well,' he said cautiously, 'it's not an easy brief.'

'I don't mean the *brief*.' Rodge's voice shook. Terry's eyes darted back to him, and he took a deep breath. 'When do *you* think they're going to tell us?'

It stunned Terry to hear Rodge speak, without feigning a

youth and fearlessness he no longer possessed. For the first time he had the sense he was talking to the real man, the man inside. 'I don't know. Maybe next week.'

'I'll probably never get another job in advertising, not after this.' At first Rodge spoke matter-of-factly, but, sentence by sentence, true emotion crept into his voice. 'How's it going to look for me? I'm thirty-six next week, you know. It's not old, but it is old. When you do what we do, it's old. Rob isn't twenty-five yet, nor Christian. Not that I've got anything against them. I've always got on fine with them, they've always liked me. They see me as a kind of big brother, I suppose. Twenty years I've been in this business. They respect that. People have to respect that. It's got to mean *something*—'

He broke off for a second to catch his breath. 'It's not Viv's fault,' he said at last. 'He's a great guy, Viv, we've always got along. But I'm – I'm just finished, that's all. I haven't got what it takes any more. It's over.'

Terry sat and watched him and said nothing.

'It's all I ever wanted to do, you know,' said Rodge haltingly. 'Ever since I was a kid.'

It was hard to know what to say after that. Rodge lapsed into a silence that said he'd expressed too many truths, and now regretted it. Terry wanted to tell him that it was all right, but knew how trite and false reassurance would sound. It wasn't all right, and both men knew it, and an hour stretched out between them like a day. When lunchtime came, Rodge didn't look at Terry as he left the meeting room to get his heat-up meal from the fridge in the kitchen. Terry got the lift down to Reception, walked through it, and out into the biting afternoon.

At the NatWest cashpoint, there was no queue. He got out his card, inserted it, pressed in his PIN number and then Balance Enquiry. Please wait, the screen told him, and the message flashed on and off for what seemed like a very long time. Then the numbers arrived and hypnotised Terry as they never had before.

You could use it to escape, Terry, the little voice whispered in his mind. *To escape with Rosina before it's too late.*

And, for the first time, he understood why he'd kept his inheritance a secret. Because it would be enough to live on for some time, wouldn't it? Enough to live on, far from Marie and Lisa and the dream – enough to escape from the increasing violence inside him.

He decided that he'd go into the club after work. He had to see Rosina.

6

'So what's happened?' asked Allie. 'Have you heard from him?'

Sitting at her desk in the warm, well-lit office, Marie squirmed inside. She couldn't bear to confess the true horror of last night, but the idea of lying to Allie seemed little better. She'd always told her sister the truth, ever since they were kids. 'He was home when I got in,' she said, longing to believe herself. 'He was really sorry. He went out to a leaving do after a work, and a friend of his got run over crossing the road. Terry had to go to the hospital with him.'

'God,' said Allie. 'Is he all right?'

'Terry's friend?' She half wanted Allie to spot the lies and demand the truth – but Allie's voice told her that she accepted every word. 'He's in a stable condition, Terry said. He should be okay.'

'That's good,' said Allie easily.

A brief silence fell – Marie was praying that the subject would be dropped, when Allie spoke again. 'Still, it was out of order of him not to call you. He could always have rung from the hospital and let you know what was going on.'

'He said he was sorry about that when I got home. Said he hadn't thought I'd be so worried.' Marie hurried over the details, hoping against hope that Allie wouldn't notice the holes in the plot. 'He seems a bit more like himself now. I think I might have been worrying about nothing.'

'Glad to hear it.'

It was never difficult to put Allie's mind at rest, Marie thought. Like her, Allie only ever wanted to believe in good things. But Marie couldn't close her eyes to the other side of life, not any more. 'Anyway, now the drama's over, you don't mind having Lise again this weekend, do you, Marie? Only you know I'm at Pontin's again and—'

'No problem. You know it's a pleasure.' And more than a pleasure now – a way of diluting the atmosphere at home, of bringing in the brightness from outside. In Marie's mind, her niece's presence was beginning to feel like a security blanket. 'I'll call round Saturday morning, same as ever. If that's okay with you.'

'Course it is,' said Allie. Then, 'Well, suppose you'd best get back to work, hadn't you? See you Saturday, Marie. I'm glad you've got all that stuff with Terry sorted out.'

'All under control,' said Marie cheerfully, and then the call was over.

So it's come to this, she thought fleetingly. I'm hiding things from Allie.

The rest of the morning slipped away, and soon it was lunchtime. On her way out to get a sandwich, she found herself alone in a lift with Robert. 'Listen,' he said, as the lift stopped, 'would you like to come for dinner next Wednesday evening? I know a nice little restaurant that's only a few minutes away.' She nodded, and smiled. 'We might as well meet up in there,' he said, and they discussed directions, and set the meeting time for seven o'clock before heading their separate ways. As Marie walked to the sandwich shop, she found herself thinking that while her relationship with Robert was the real secret, her relationship with Terry felt like it.

Back in the office, the quiet afternoon passed too quickly. She didn't want to go home: she saw herself sitting at the kitchen table in five hours' time, dreading her husband's return yet simultaneously dreading his continued absence. In the end-of-day management meeting, the head of Finance droned on as interminably as ever, but this time her unwillingness to meet Robert's eyes across the table had nothing to do with the fear of laughter. Rather, she feared the lack of it, seeing Robert's *moue* of theatrical despair, and knowing that the prospect of home and Terry blocked out humour.

When the meeting was over, she went into her office to get her umbrella, but she couldn't bring herself to head straight out, and told herself she had to check her e-mails. She sat at her desk and went through the messages again – neat enclosed boxes on the luminous screen – someone's leaving drinks tomorrow night in the Central Bar, suggestions invited for the Christmas party's fancy-dress theme. She'd like to have stayed longer, but could imagine half past seven turning to half past nine too clearly. Like a woman facing up to a lifelong fear, she rose from her desk. Already, she could feel the icy chill outside in her bones, the pitch black sky and the rattling tube carriages, a journey home that lasted for ever, and not long enough.

7

He's back, thought Rosina. I knew he would be.

She stood by the bar and watched Terry approach. She'd find out what he thought of her tonight. Whether she was really all-important to him or— 'Hello,' she said.

'Do you want to sit down?'

'Of course.' The words of their greeting had taken on a ritual quality; his cautious formality pleased her. 'I have to, if we're going to leave together. You know that.'

They went to a table by the dance-floor and she watched Karl hurry over. 'Good evening, sir. Would you like to see the champagne menu?'

'No, thanks. We'll just have the Lanson.' Karl walked away. When Rosina was sure that he was out of earshot, she leaned in closer to Terry and spoke quietly. 'Where does she think you go in the evenings? Julia?'

'I tell her I'm working late. I don't know what she *thinks*.'

'Doesn't she tell you?'

'She never says anything. Not to me.'

'Do you want her to?'

'I used to.'

Under the ever-moving points of light from the disco globe, she watched him intently. The half-hidden anger in his eyes had never intrigued her more and drew her like a glimpse of bare flesh. She wanted to see his anger naked. 'So she doesn't care about you at all?'

'I thought I told you that a while ago.'

'Maybe I forgot,' she lied. Her eyes never left his. 'But you love her.'

'I told you what I thought about her. I told you she's a bitch.'

'A part of you loves her.'

'A part of me used to.'

'Doesn't she matter to you at all?'

'No,' he said. 'Not any more.'

How hard it was to get to the truth of him. He answered questions, but still a part of him was locked away from her, a shadowy part, the part that drew her. The part that reminded her of herself. Karl brought the champagne and left. She barely noticed him. Suddenly, she realised that the question in her mind was a simple one after all.

'Do I matter to you?'

'Of course you do. You know you do.'

She knew instinctively that he was telling the truth and tried not to let the rush of private, complacent joy show in her eyes. 'Prove it,' she said, and knew she sounded as cool and offhand as she always did.

'All right.'

His words took her by surprise; she looked at him closely. 'How?'

'I've got something to ask you,' he answered her obliquely. 'Back at the hotel.'

'Why not here?'

'It doesn't feel right.'

He sounded as if he was about to propose, but she knew it wouldn't be that. Not marriage, but something important to him. She tried to get some clue from the expression in his eyes, but it had never been harder to interpret – tension was all she could see, a kind of half-suppressed urgency. They finished the champagne without speaking, watching one another as voices and laughter from other tables drifted around them. Karl returned, and Terry handed over his credit card.

'Well,' she said, when Karl had gone.

'I'll see you outside Austin Reed,' he said quietly. 'In five minutes.'

'Like always. I know.' She smiled, rose from the table, walked away. In the deserted ladies', she touched up her makeup. Cold blue eyes watched her intently from the mirror, and she wondered what Terry was going to ask her.

8

'There's a cab,' said Rosina. 'Just coming now.'

They flagged it down easily, and climbed in. Terry gave his instructions to the driver and sat back.

The chaotic beauty of the city in darkness had never struck Terry more intensely than now: it combined with the enormity of the immediate future to overwhelm him. In Piccadilly, towering banks of electric signs promised a good-fellowship that the bleak streets below them denied, while horns and sirens blared and screamed from all sides. Trafalgar Square had never seemed so huge or so forbidding, still black water glinting before the vastness of Nelson's Column. Unforgettable images passed him through the glass as Rosina's hand brushed his. He'd thought London was a cold town once, he remembered, but he knew better now.

Are you going to ask her, Terry? Are you really going to ask her?

In the hotel foyer, the greasy man on Reception showed no sign of recognition, and Terry paid by card as he always did. In the bright lights and the silence, the pen scratched loudly on the paper. 'Room 120,' the man said, doling out the chunky room key. 'Third floor. Lift's working now.'

Terry stepped into the lift with Rosina. The doors wheezed shut behind them. Longing overcame him like nostalgia – he seized her in his arms and they kissed. As they rose, he saw her back reflected in the wall mirror. Her hair glinted a strangely artificial blue-black in the institutional light that seemed to come from everywhere and nowhere, and he watched intimacy and impersonality blend into something erotic beyond definition.

In the hotel room, they made hungry, wordless love as soon as the door had closed behind them. Her perfume intoxicated him and he sensed the darkness unwinding endlessly beyond them with something beyond conscious thought. Its freedom and amorality were so much like hers. 'Rosina,' he murmured into her neck, 'Rosina,' and then the world exploded.

They lay together, still partially clothed, on the bed, flesh brushing flesh in unexpected places. She stirred in his arms to smile up at him. 'Well?'

He felt as if he'd just stepped off a hell-for-leather fairground ride, before he remembered – impossible, he thought, that he could have forgotten his imminent request. 'I don't know how to say it. I don't know how to ask it.'

'Just say it. Just ask it.'

'You'll think I'm mad. *Insane.*'

'Maybe not,' she said, and laughed. 'Just ask me.'

Her laughter affected him like a drug – cruel, childish, unselfconscious: the sound of liberty. It broke down his last doubts, and replaced his apprehension with calm, and a sense of peace he remembered too strongly from the terrible dream.

'I'm leaving everything, soon,' he said. '*Escaping* everything. And I want you to come with me.'

9

'Where to?' she asked. 'And when?'

'I don't know. Soon.' He found it impossible to read her expression and spoke quickly, desperately. 'Would you?'

'Why not?'

Her enigmatic smile confused him as much as her throwaway tone. 'Really?'

'Of course,' she said, and laughed again. 'Why do you look so surprised?'

'I don't know.' It seemed important to make sure she hadn't misunderstood him, to make sure that she'd really agreed. 'So you will?'

'For the last time, *yes*.'

He couldn't quite believe that she'd understood the enormity of his request – but of course she had, she understood everything. Leaving it all behind didn't matter to her as it did to him, because she was free, and she always had been.

'It'll be soon,' he said eventually. 'Maybe two weeks. I don't know yet.'

Her shoulders rose and fell. 'Will we be staying in Britain . . . ?'

'Yeah. I don't know where yet. I'll think of somewhere.'

'Two weeks, then,' she said, reflectively. 'Don't worry. I'll come with you. Of course I'll come with you.'

He'd expected questions about why he wanted to escape and what he was so desperate to escape from – was prepared to unburden himself of at least some of his terrors, if not the ones that really mattered – but as the seconds stretched out, he realised she wasn't going to ask him anything. Again, he felt she was his salvation, all-knowing, all-understanding. 'I'll tell you more,' he said. 'Soon. I just wanted to know if you would.'

'So now you know.'

'I thought you'd say yes. I hoped, anyway.' They lay together for a little while longer. Then he disengaged his flesh from hers. 'I'm going to have to go. I don't want her getting suspicious.'

'Of course,' she said, and smiled. 'Julia.'

In the harsh lights of the tiny bathroom, he showered, dried himself and dressed. When he came out, the bedroom seemed darker and more enticing them ever. Rosina's silhouette in the bed inspired longing and anticipation – he wanted her to be a constant presence in his life and soon she would be. 'I'll come in to see you again tomorrow night,' he said. 'At the club.'

'Okay,' she said, and curled up in bed. Her pale blue eyes watched him over the bedclothes. ''Bye, then.'

Out of the room, Terry took the lift to the ground floor. A middle-aged man in a lightweight suit as crumpled as his face was arguing with the greasy man on Reception. 'I mean, we're only going to be half an hour,' he was complaining. 'It's ridiculous that I've got to pay . . .' A blonde girl in platform sandals watched him, with an air of bored and infinite contempt. Terry barely noticed them. He went out into the night.

The future filled his mind as he walked. Car headlights splashed around him and he tasted dizzy joy at the prospect of escaping this city, this life, the woman he'd married. Of escaping a huge suppressed violence that was moving closer and closer with every day. Nobody would miss him, and vanishing seemed to be the only way to stop that dream coming true. He could feel himself teetering on the edge of a precipice just as he had twenty-seven years ago. Soon, he thought, he might not be able to stop himself—

Escape and Rosina. As the bright lights of Victoria approached, those two things were all he had left to believe in, and he clung to them. Surely, with escape and Rosina in his mind, he'd be able to keep his new anger under control for a couple of weeks – *surely.*

Are you sure about that, Terry? Are you absolutely certain?

The little voice was more insistent than ever, and he forced it away as he walked onto the concourse. Things wouldn't get out of hand, he told himself, over the next fourteen days. He went through the ticket barrier, waited for the train and boarded. As the train set off, he sat and gazed out of the window. A pallid ghost of himself stared back from the familiar darkness, somehow blended with the office blocks, and the crawling trail of headlights, and the bank of tiny lights that glittered like a childhood memory far away.

10

Marie lay sleepless between crisp clean sheets that smelt of fabric-softener. The luminous numbers on the bedside clock-radio said it was eleven thirty. Tonight, the darkness had an unearthly quality, she thought. Like being alone in space.
Don't think about Terry. Think about Robert.

She tried but the two men's images seemed inextricably linked. She thought of Robert's laughter and remembered Terry's silence over breakfast, thought of Robert's warm, easy smile and wondered where Terry was tonight, what he was doing. Images of her husband haunted her, flashing in and out of one another like a frenetic rock video. The cup of tea flying across the room on the evening when he'd *snapped* at her. The thin rectangle of golden light round the closed study door. Endless photographs of a sweet-faced little girl unravelling an enigmatic past – Terry's fury as he'd grabbed the album—

The madness in his eyes before he'd left.

Stop being so ridiculous, she told herself. It was anger, you were both angry, you'd had a serious row – but it was like one frightened woman reassuring another, and the words held no conviction. A sixth sense told her that his expression had been far beyond any anger in the world and, at least inside, she knew it as well as she did her own name.

Then she heard the front door open downstairs.

Terror overcame her as she heard Terry close and bolt it, heard the first creaking footsteps on the stairs. She wanted to call out to him, if only to break the oppressive silence, then an even deeper fear forced its hand over her mouth. She turned over so that she was facing away from the door, pushed her face half into the pillow and squeezed her eyes tightly shut. She waited for him to come in.

The small familiar noises from the bathroom seemed to go on for ever – the distant sound of running water through a closed door, the almost inaudible murmur of teeth being vigorously brushed. *What are you frightened of?* a querulous voice demanded in her mind. *Why don't you just call out to him?* But she had no rational answer. All she knew was that she was afraid to be alone with her husband in the dark, and she pretended to be asleep so that she wouldn't have to face him.

The bathroom door opened. Footsteps on the landing. The bedroom door creaked. He was there.

Marie pushed her face harder into the pillow and heard him walking round the bed, his bare feet on the carpet. He was coming round to her side, and his quiet breathing filled the world – white spots exploded behind her closed eyelids, her heartbeat pounded in her ears like heavy rain. She breathed in the sweet, cloying smell of fabric-softener, and knew, in a moment of freezing terror, that he was standing over her, looking down at her and it felt like being watched by a dangerous stranger.

Thick, oppressive silence. His breathing close. Each second that passed intensified her fear a little more, and it fed off itself to become something like hysteria. *What's he thinking about?* she wondered wildly. *He's been staring down at me for minutes, now, what can he be thinking about?* And then she couldn't stand the uncertainty any longer, and stirred and muttered, as if she was about to wake from deep sleep. Infinite relief overcame her as she heard him take a sharp breath, and walk round the bed to his own side.

The mattress creaked as he climbed in, and she felt him beside her – her flesh seemed to shrink away from his. Although he fell asleep quickly, she'd never felt less like sleeping in her life. That long silence as she'd felt him watching her screamed in her mind, on and on through the night, a nameless nocturnal horror that crept out and gibbered from dark corners. Beside her, Terry stirred uneasily, but his face wore an expression of absolute peace. As she looked at him, the secrets of his life obsessed her – what he'd been thinking of as he'd gazed down at her, what he was dreaming of now.

11

She didn't ask him where he'd been last night. Not even over breakfast, when there was nothing else to discuss. She just set down his coffee without speaking, looked out of the window, at her nails, anywhere but at him. He sat and sipped in a silence that filled the world until he left for work.

He didn't know why her indifference surprised him. For two full days now, he'd known she didn't care about him any more, and the knowledge tasted like bitter, sneaking relief. It didn't matter that he was planning to escape, not to her. She probably wouldn't give a damn when he vanished without a trace. Or perhaps she'd even be pleased.

On the tube into Tottenham Court Road, he stood in a compress of strangers and thought about Rosina – the texture of her skin, the sound of her laughter. He would go into the club and see her that night. Soon they'd be away together. Somewhere far from here . . .

Think about anything, Terry. Just not the dream. And not last night. You were very close to the edge last night, you know. When you were looking down at Marie. In the dark.

I wouldn't have done anything, he told the voice desperately. *I was just watching her.*

Are you sure, Terry? the voice asked implacably, and he jerked back to the present tense, the word 'escape' repeating in his head like a mantra.

When he walked into the office, Rob, Alex and Lucy were already there. They clustered round Rob's desk and talked in carrying whispers. Before he had time to take in what they were saying, he passed Rodge's desk and stopped dead. The stress-relief toy and the football pennant, the sketch-pad and the artist's pens had gone. The desk was bare.

'He got his cards yesterday evening,' Alex was saying, and laughed. 'Stupid old fart. Viv got him to stay late, then called him into his office and—'

'All right, Terry?' called Lucy, as she caught sight of him. 'How's it going?'

It was glaringly obvious that she'd spoken solely to alert the lads to his arrival. All conversation stopped around Rob's desk, and Terry found himself watched intently. Rob's awkwardness was as chilling as Alex's thinly-veiled smirk, and Lucy's impassivity. He took off his coat. 'Morning,' he replied, and the voice he heard didn't sound like his own.

There was nowhere to go but the kitchen. He filled the kettle and waited for it to boil, trying not to look at the photograph on the noticeboard. A sense of finality filled his mind. With Rodge's dismissal, his last link with this world had been severed and, far from being a beguiling daydream, escape had become as inevitable as death. When he was made redundant in hours or days, there'd be nothing to hold him back.

'Suppose you've heard about Rodge.'

He turned. It was Rob. Rob wore the expression of someone doggedly doing the right thing – embarrassed, determined, solemn. 'Yeah,' said Terry quietly. 'I've heard.'

'Fucking shame, mate. He was all right,' said Rob, and the

look in his eyes said he knew Terry would soon follow in Rodge's footsteps, and that he knew that Terry knew it, and that he wasn't comfortable with office politics. His shoulders rose and fell. 'Well, see you back in there,' he said, and was gone, back to the noisy desk and the table-football and the glittering future, where his genuine regret would soon fade in the light.

The kettle boiled. Terry poured water over the brown granules in his mug with a hand that was as steady as rock. The unthinkable had arrived, and he looked it full in the face, and found it didn't matter. Now, prospects and ambition had never existed. All there was consisted of last night and the dream and Rosina – the need to escape from the violence inside him before it was too late.

12

Marie kept thinking about going out with Robert next Wednesday night. She told herself she thought about it because she knew it would be wonderful, but while that wasn't exactly a lie, it was a long way from the whole truth. It was a decoy, pure and simple, which distracted her attention from last night. A self-defence mechanism that stopped her wondering what Terry had been thinking of as he'd stood, statue-still, looking down at her.

Even in the familiar lights of her office, she could recall the taste of terror too vividly. How clearly she'd remember it that night, God only knew. She saw herself in eight hours' time, and it felt like a premonition – lying in a well-decorated, familiar bedroom, that had taken on shades of menace, exhausted beside her sleeping husband, but fighting back exhaustion like an enemy. If she gave in to it, he might wake, walk round the bed and look down at her for endless minutes, and she wouldn't know anything about it.

At lunchtime, she walked to the sandwich shop with Sandra – chatting with her didn't seem unprofessional now, and she wondered why it had once seemed important. Nothing mattered any more. The prospect of going back to Terry sucked the colour out of everything. 'Are you coming to the Central Bar tonight?' Sandra asked, as they went back to work. 'It's Gemma's leaving do.'

'I know,' said Marie. 'I saw the e-mail. I probably will, if I don't have to work too late.'

In the event, she did – not out of any desire to socialise and chatter but because she didn't want to go home. She tried not to acknowledge it, tried to pretend to herself that she really wanted to be at the party. But the loud music and shrieking voices troubled her, and the laughter maddened her like ignorance. Everyone else in this room, she thought, would return home without thinking twice about it, would fall asleep without realising how lucky they were. Alone in this crowded bar, she had Terry, and fear, and the overwhelming loneliness of secrecy.

There was no comfort here, but she couldn't bear to leave, and stayed on after Sandra, Trish and the girls from Credit had all gone home. She wished Robert was there, but he wasn't. At the bar, she stood and sipped her wine and talked to Carol Ellis about the Christmas party.

'Everyone's being so apathetic about the theme,' Carol complained. 'We've had hardly any suggestions.'

Marie smiled a sympathetic smile she didn't feel. She felt like a child taking refuge in an uncomfortable hiding-place, knowing deep inside that there was no delaying the inevitable, that the future had to be faced. Finally, at nine thirty, she knew there was no point in hanging on. 'Look at the time. I'd better be off,' she said to Carol. 'See you tomorrow.'

'Okay. Have a good night, Marie.'

'You too.' She did a brief tour of the room to say goodbye to the hangers-on, tasting warmth and normality with a mixture of relish and despair. Then she was stepping out of the bar, alone, heading back to a nightmare, longing for Wednesday evening and Robert.

13

Rosina stood by the bar and smiled. 'Hello,' she said.

'Do you want to sit down?'

'You don't have to ask me that, any more.'

The club was quiet tonight, and they were the first couple to take a table. Karl was with them almost immediately.

'We'll have the Lanson,' Terry said.

She watched Karl nod and smile and walk away, and returned her attention to Terry. In his pale, enigmatic eyes, she could see herself clearly reflected, and realised he saw her as she'd always wanted him to: as the club incarnate. He didn't need to look around him any more, she thought. The darkness and the fascination were all in her.

He leaned closer to her. 'We're going next Friday night,' he said quietly.

'What? *Escaping everything?*' She wondered what he'd think if he could read her mind – his expression said he didn't understand her, and it overwhelmed her with tenderness and cruelty. 'Does it scare you? Hearing me say it out loud like that?'

He shook his head. 'Nothing matters to you, does it?'

'Christine said that once,' she said idly, and then Karl came over with the champagne. 'Where are we going to go?' she asked, when he had gone.

'Anywhere. I don't know. I'll think of somewhere over the next few days.'

'And how long for?'

'For *ever.* You know that.'

'Oh, of course,' she said, and smiled. 'For *ever.*'

It was like a toast in the thin, rosy lights: they clicked their glasses together, and drank. Her gaze panned across the dancers: Vicki and the other girls sitting and smoking by the bar, the first few couples now at the tables. 'It doesn't matter,' she said, 'I'm not going to miss anything here,' and they sat and drank without speaking for a while longer.

'What will you do?' she asked at last. 'Come round to collect me?'

'It's the best way. I'll need your address.'

'Now?'

It seemed as if her recklessness had infected him – he spoke almost flippantly: 'It's as good a time as any.'

'All right.'

She reached into her bag and pulled out a chipped black biro. A small cardboard notice in the middle of the table said that tips could be given at your discretion, and were not compulsory – she picked it up and scrawled something on the back, then handed it to him. 'My address,' she said gravely. 'With directions.'

She watched him glance at it, maybe thinking that her writing wasn't quite what he'd expected. She disliked her handwriting and always had – in some way she couldn't quite pinpoint, it seemed to express the truth of herself. She was relieved to see him tucking it away in his wallet. 'I'll come round,' he said. 'Then we can escape together.'

Music pulsed and the disco lights turned the champagne in their glasses from red to silver to gold. Eventually, clumsily, he spoke. 'I won't be coming in here again before we leave. I don't want her to get any more suspicious than she already is. If there's another argument – if she *starts* another argument . . .'

His unexpected weakness warmed her – his petty fears, so much like Christine's, made her feel all-powerful. She spoke mockingly: 'You're scared of her, aren't you?'

'I'm scared of what might happen.'

There was something in his eyes that she interpreted as

cowardice and her smile widened. 'No wonder you want to *escape*,' she said, 'for *ever*.' Lights whirled and dancers writhed and his fear was fun, just as the world was, these days. 'Do you want to go back to the hotel tonight?'

'You know I do.'

'Good,' she said. 'So do I.'

14

He stood outside the windows of Austin Reed and waited for her. The mannequins stared out at him from behind the glass, became something more than inanimate figures as he looked back – as pale and expressionless as she was, as icily impervious to human emotion – and a glittering river of traffic flowed on and on behind him, and he saw its reflection in the windows. It had been no more than two months ago that he'd come here for the first time. He wondered how it had all come down to this so quickly, and understood that he didn't know and didn't care.

Her footsteps rang out sharply on the pavement. He turned to watch her approach. She reached him quickly and they fell into step together.

'There's a taxi,' she said, and he flagged it down.

In the back of the cab he watched her gaze out of the window. There was, he thought, something unreal about her beauty, white skin, black hair and blue eyes, the kind of colouring you read and fantasised about but rarely saw in life.

'What are you thinking about?' she asked.

'Nothing.' Lights from passing cars moved over her face and hair, streaking them red, orange and white. 'I just can't work you out.'

'Maybe I don't want you to.' Her laughter had never excited him as it did now. Something cold and artificial stirred in its cadences; a skilled actress, a cruel child, a girl whose mystery defied definition. And he seized her and kissed her deeply, and Piccadilly, Trafalgar Square and Whitehall rose and fell around them as they kissed on through the night.

In the hotel foyer, Terry handed over his credit card, signed in and the greasy man doled out the key. 'Second floor,' he said, 'lift's over there.' They walked over to the lift and got in, and the doors slid together behind them.

They didn't touch until the door of the room had swung shut, and then the world narrowed to stark physical need. There was no need for preliminaries or conversation tonight. There was no need for thought. There was no need for anything beyond immediate sensation – her raw-silk skin and little sounds of pleasure, the prospect of freedom and salvation becoming the ultimate aphrodisiac.

'Rosina,' he murmured, and she cried out sharply and gripped him with her thighs, 'Rosina,' and the intensity of his pleasure became almost unendurable, and Julia Fielding's face filled his mind in the split second before the world shattered.

Then it was over, and he was lying in her arms.

'I'm going to have to go,' he said eventually. 'I should be at home.'

'It doesn't matter,' she said. 'You won't have to run back to Julia for a long time. For *ever*.'

It amazed him that she could sound so flippant, but she always amazed him. He went into the bathroom, showered, and put on his clothes. When he came out, he found that the warmth and safety of the bed no longer pulled at him, because soon he'd be able to have as much of it as he wanted. There was only a week of indifferent eyes and terror left.

'I'll be round next Friday night,' he said, from the door. 'Probably around seven. I can't say for sure.'

'I'll look forward to seeing you,' she murmured, and her laughter followed him out of the room, into the lift, through Reception, out into the night where he waited for a taxi with a timebomb ticking in his mind.

15

Rosina lay in bed, listening to the erratic dripping of water in the bathroom, and the constant murmur of traffic beyond the window. She was smiling.

You don't care about anything, do you, Rosina? said pathetic little Christine, and Terry said, *Nothing matters to you, does it?* and a cold thrill ran through her as she realised that then and now had become the same. She'd been right to persist with this relationship – the excitement that filled her made it all worthwhile.

'Rosina,' he'd groaned into her neck as he approached his climax, 'Rosina,' and the helpless need in his voice had triggered hers. Again, she was a part of the world that had dismissed her in disgrace seven years ago, when she was sixteen – Parker Bailey and the beautiful house in Chelsea, the glamorous silver-framed parents and the white-and-pinewood bedroom all boiled down to power, after all. Then, she hadn't known it was so straightforward. But now she knew more. And it was.

'I'm escaping everything,' he'd said, 'and I want you to come with me.' He was so silly, she thought, just as Christine had been, back at school. She supposed she should feel sorry for his wife, but she didn't feel anything for the unseen Julia Fielding. She wasn't part of the equation, Rosina thought, she didn't matter at all. What mattered was that he wanted and needed her more than anything in the world. That he believed every word she said.

He doesn't know me as well as he thinks, Rosina reflected, and wondered if anything could be more intoxicating than power and secrecy combined. She knew everything about him, but had never allowed him to get the slightest glimpse of her true self – her thoughts and motivations, and what she'd really done to get herself sent away. She moved in the shadows, and he'd never really seen *her* at all.

In the night, you could say anything. You could be anyone.

She lay in bed and thought about escaping the city with him. The darkness of a stranger's room enfolded and caressed her. The tap in the bathroom dripped on and on, marking out the seconds as faint sirens rose and fell through the night.

16

Even though he didn't care about losing his job any more, Terry still couldn't help wondering when the bullet would be fired – when a solemn-eyed Viv Sacker would appear at his desk and ask him if he had a minute, if he could come into his office. It was, he thought, like Chinese water torture. The drop of water didn't matter, but the timing did.

It was late in the afternoon, and the windows showed it was already getting dark – the office lights were too bright, and seemed more artificial than ever. Rodge's empty desk reminded Terry that soon he'd also be gone from here. It evoked too much – Rosina, escape, freedom – and brought fear and exhilaration in rolling waves. He wondered when they'd take away Rodge's computer, and whether he'd be here to see them do it, and felt his own time here running out. Laughter rang out from the table-football, where Rob played Alex, and Christian and Lucy watched them, and talked.

'When do you reckon Viv's going to call a meeting?' asked Lucy.

'Fuck knows,' said Christian. Then, more quietly, 'Not over *yet*, is it?'

'We're going to have to get a freelancer in, when it's all over,' complained Alex from the table. 'Can't manage this workload, when it's just us.'

'Yeah – rushed off your feet, aren't you, mate?' called Christian, and they all laughed.

Terry sat and listened to them, but they didn't matter to

him any more. *Next Friday*, he thought, *I'll be away from all of it, everything'll be all right, I'll be safe.* Between now and then, all he had to do was control his hatred and loneliness, try to avoid confrontational situations that might unleash them. It should be easy, with only eight days left.

What if Marie starts an argument with you, Terry? Will you be able to control yourself, then?

Of course he would. He'd just burrow deeper inside himself, to a place in his mind where there was nothing but a hotel room, and red neon lights through a mist of rain, and the sound of Rosina's laughter. Reach a point where Marie and her indifference simply ceased to exist.

I will *be safe soon*, he repeated desperately in his mind. *Finally safe. With Rosina, I'll be safe.*

When five thirty came, Alex and Lucy were the first to leave, and he had the deep-rooted sense that Sacker was going to come over to him now – he had come over to Rodge at the end of the day. Resignation crept over him as he saw the man emerge from his office, intensified, then faded – Sacker was wearing his coat, carrying his briefcase, bypassing Terry's desk. 'Night-night, boys and girls,' he called, 'have a marvellous weekend,' and then he was gone. And Terry felt something like disappointment. More than anything now, he wanted this part of his life to be closed, over.

He yearned to go to the club and see Rosina, but the idea of sparking off Marie's cold fury killed the urge stone dead: each night the dream reminded him of what *that* might lead to. He'd have to go straight home every night, now. Rob and Christian left together, a couple of others separately. Terry got up and put on his coat. It didn't bother him that nobody said goodbye. All that mattered was keeping his temper, biding his time, waiting on tenterhooks for next Friday night.

The lift that took him down to Reception was empty. He walked out of the main double doors into the evening. At Tottenham Court Road station, he went through the ticket barrier. He stood on the escalator in a forest of strangers, and felt the city taking him home.

17

Marie sat across from Terry at the kitchen table, and ate mechanically. The prospect of the coming night weighed on her mind, the talcum-scented shadows and the paranoid terror of sleep. She didn't want to speak, but suddenly had to. 'We need to talk, Terry.'

His eyes moves to meet hers. Secrets stirred in their pale depths more furtively and obviously than ever. 'What about?'

It infuriated her that he could still pretend nothing was wrong. 'What do you think?' she demanded. '*Us*, of course.'

'What about us?'

'Oh, for God's sake.' She reined in her fear, confusion and anger with a great effort. 'You know something's wrong, just like I do. There's no point pretending it's nothing.'

His voice was rational, polite. 'I don't know what you mean.'

'Yes, you do. Why don't you ever talk to me? Why don't you tell me what you're doing?'

'I've just been preoccupied with work. I've told you that already.' There was something unnatural about his glassy calm. In another man, she might have suspected drugs, but she knew Terry wouldn't touch them. 'It won't last much longer, this busy time. It's cooling off now.'

Silence fell again, and the clock ticked on the wall. Marie wanted to believe him, but no matter how she tried, it was impossible. She forced herself to say what had to be said. 'You know perfectly well. It's not just that.'

His voice was so quiet, it was almost inaudible. 'You never use my name any more, do you?'

She stared at him. 'What's *that* supposed to mean?'

'Nothing.' It was as if he was speaking from a drugged Valium dream. 'It doesn't matter.'

His passivity frightened her almost as much as his hatred had – again she wondered if he was going through a mental breakdown. Try as she might, she couldn't stop herself speaking as she did. 'I can't stand much more of this. If we can't get on, maybe we should think about splitting up.'

'Is that what you want?'

'I don't know,' she said cautiously and quietly. 'I really don't know.'

Neither spoke after that for several minutes. Marie sat and ate, hearing the wind behind the blinds, cutlery on plates in the kitchen's near-silence. When they'd finished dinner, Terry went into the living room and put on the telly. She stayed in the kitchen and washed up.

18

'Guess what?' said Allie. 'I've definitely got that cruise-ship booking for next March. That's a whole month, Marie. And the money's fantastic.'

'Great.' Sitting in Allie's living-room, Marie sipped her tea. 'When did you find out?'

'Yesterday. They called me in the evening. You might have to look after Lisa mind. I won't be able to take her along.'

'That's all right.'

'You sure?' Allie looked at Marie with her eyebrows raised. 'You sound a bit unimpressed.'

'Oh, no. It's not you, Allie. It's just—'

'Just what? I thought you had all that stuff with Terry sorted out.'

'I have,' she lied. 'I'm just in a funny mood today. Probably PMT.' She wasn't sure that Allie believed her and hurried on, before vague scepticism could turn into something more concrete. 'But I'm really pleased for you, Allie. Honestly.'

'I know.' Allie smiled.

It was like watching a party through a window, happiness both visible and unattainable, laughing faces through thick glass. She couldn't join in her sister's good mood, Marie realised. Not now.

Allie talked a little more about the cruise-ship booking and what it would involve, while Marie sat and smiled and listened, and accepted Allie's offer of more tea. This flat was so bright and welcoming, she thought. It should have been impossible to feel alone or frightened here, but she did.

'What are you getting Mum for her birthday next month?' asked Allie.

'I don't know.' The date had slipped Marie's mind, and she struggled to pretend that it hadn't. 'Something for the house, I suppose.'

'Yeah, me, too. You going to see them before Christmas?'

'I expect so.' But she couldn't think of anything apart from her husband and her marriage and how it was all going wrong. 'I'll see how it goes.'

Lisa came in with her overnight bag and they talked for a little longer. 'We'd better be off, anyway,' Marie said eventually. 'See you Monday, Allie. Come on, Lisa.' And an image of Terry's closed-off eyes flashed in her mind as they left.

19

On Sunday morning, Terry came into the kitchen. Marie was chatting with Lisa at the table, and neither acknowledged his entrance. The sky beyond the window was pregnant with dark-grey stormclouds – the light was yellowish, apocalyptic.

In the fridge, the last carton of orange juice was unopened. He set it down on the side, and went to the cutlery drawer. The sound as it opened seemed very loud, but Marie and Lisa didn't appear to notice it.

'You haven't got much of an appetite this morning, poppet,' Marie was murmuring. 'Come on, have a bit more.'

He saw the sharp butcher's knife that Marie used for carving roasts as a thin dull gleam at the back of the drawer. The sight of it hypnotised him as her soothing voice flowed around him – a gentle, caring, maternal voice that Julia Fielding had never used with him. How easy it would be to take out that knife now. Lisa's head bowed obediently over her cornflakes, her sand-coloured ponytail falling over one shoulder, leaving her neck bare—

Did she scream, Terry? Did Katie have time to scream?

The little voice hit him like a rush of freezing water. He got out a little pair of scissors, slammed the drawer so hard that Marie and Lisa both looked round at once. 'What was that?' asked Marie sharply.

'Just the drawer. It was stuck.' Terry snipped open the carton of juice, poured himself a glass and sat down at the table with his wife and niece. He left the scissors on the side. He couldn't bring himself to open that drawer again and look inside. It had felt like teetering on the edge of a precipice.

You have to escape, Terry, the ever-present voice stated quietly. *You're a danger to them for as long as you stay here. A real danger. And you know it.*

I'm going on Friday. That's only six days away. No time at all.

No, the voice replied, *but it's long enough,* and Terry forced it away.

Marie picked up Lisa's bowl, 'There's a good girl,' Terry heard her say, 'I knew you could finish them,' and she stood up to wash it in the sink. Lisa's huge grey eyes moved to her uncle, and she watched him without speaking.

He'd always sensed that Lisa could read his thoughts, but never quite as intensely as now – her pale, watchful little face wore an expression of understanding, judgement, distance, pity. He rose abruptly from the table. 'Just going for a shower,' he said, and left the kitchen.

He spent most of Saturday avoiding them – cutting back a bush in the back garden, going down to the local shop for some more gravy granules when Marie said she'd run out – but when it got dark there was nothing left to do, and nowhere left to go except the living-room and the kitchen. They ate dinner together, and Marie fussed over Lisa. Terry tried not to meet the child's eyes, and kept his thoughts fixed on the following Friday. After that, they watched television together for a couple of hours, and at half past eight, Marie went upstairs with Lisa to put her to bed.

When she came down and sat beside him on the sofa, he didn't take her hand – he never did any more: it was pointless seeking reassurance from someone when you knew they didn't care. She didn't take his, either. They sat side by side, looking at the screen, not saying a word. Terry became sure, when she spoke, it would be about splitting up again, but, in the event, it wasn't.

'Wonder how Allie's been getting on tonight.'

He thought of Katie lying dead in an orchard, his mother's face when he'd told her. 'Who knows?'

'I really hope it works out for her, you know. She could do with a break.'

She's got a lot more than that to worry about, murmured the voice, *and she'll know it soon, if you don't get out, Terry. If only for a couple of seconds, she'll know it—*

The words came out of nowhere, and startled him. His shoulders rose and fell in a semblance of near-indifference. 'She'll be all right,' he said. 'Everything'll be all right.' The lamplight hung heavily around them, yellowish, oppressive. They sat side by side and watched TV for a while longer before going to bed.

20

The first days of Terry's last week in this familiar world felt strange: in one sense, they lasted for ever; in another, they passed in a blur. On Monday, he was convinced that the axe would fall, and the moment never came, but neither did the departmental meeting that he knew would mark the official end of the purge. On Tuesday, another art director was made redundant, a colourless woman named Chloë, who'd started quite recently, and to whom Terry had spoken maybe five times. He couldn't grieve for her, but the news of her redundancy seemed important. Deep down, he knew he was next, and that Viv Sacker was going to tell him so on Wednesday.

On Monday and Tuesday, he walked to NatWest in his lunch-hour and looked at the numbers on the screen – he'd chipped into his inheritance with his visits to the club, but there was still more than enough for a year or so's freedom. And after that he'd find another job, nothing to do with advertising. Even though it seemed impossible here with Rosina, anything could be possible – she carried salvation in her every word and movement. When he was alone with her, far from this city, the future would look good again. To him she'd become more than a girl who lived, breathed and talked: a symbol of liberty and hope, an allegorical figure.

In the evenings, he returned to Marie, watched her look straight through him, and waited for her to allude to separation. It was as inevitable as his quiet invitation into Sacker's office – but on Monday night and Tuesday night, she didn't say another word about it. When she spoke to him, it was always about the domestic and the specific – the rubbish that needed taking out, what was on ITV later, what the managing director had said to her that afternoon. Yet he thought her eyes were preoccupied, and that maybe her remarks were a smokescreen for deeper, darker concerns.

The December weather had deteriorated into dark mornings and almost constrant drizzle – they had to put on the kitchen lights to have breakfast, and he sat and sipped his coffee in a rosy glow that reminded him of the club. Sat and sipped, trying to forget about the dream he now had every night without fail, about the cutlery drawer and Julia Fielding, and the way that his mind was fraying. He thought about Rosina.

The words repeated in his head like a mantra. *Till Friday. Till Friday.*

21

At five forty-five on Wednesday evening the office was almost empty, and the lads and Lucy had long since deserted the table-football for a pint in a nearby pub. The silence was broken only by a solitary copywriter typing up headlines in a corner. Terry was about to turn off his computer and get his coat when Sacker walked out of his office, came over to him.

'Terry?' he asked quietly. 'Have you got a moment?'

It was exactly what Terry had known he'd say before he broke the news. The moment had arrived. Terry felt relieved that Rob, Christian and Alex weren't around to watch him follow Sacker into his office. Even now that it all meant nothing, he wouldn't have wanted that.

In Sacker's overcrowded inner sanctum, Terry sat down across the desk, and suddenly wanted to get the ritual over with. 'It's the redundancies, isn't it?' he asked, and Sacker nodded slowly, sadly.

How devastating this would have been two months ago, Terry thought. Then he had longed for this office – the creative director's desk, framed ads on the wall, a seat at the industry awards every year. Now, it seemed insubstantial, and Rosina's image drained it of resonance. 'I'm sorry, Terry,' Sacker was saying, smooth voice parading in sympathy, 'but you'll almost certainly he happier working somewhere else. The culture here's moving on from what it used to be, as I'm sure you've noticed. Maybe you could team up with Rodge again.'

'Maybe.' Terry had no intention of discussing his future plans with this man, or pretending that this industry was still important to him. He saw Sacker taking in his impassivity, probably thinking him shell-shocked by the news. 'Well,' said Terry at last, 'that's it, then.'

'Of course, you'll receive two months' salary as severance pay, as per your contract.' Sacker sounded pleased to be moving away from the emotive side of things – his voice was now brisk, businesslike. 'It'll go into your current account at the end of the month, as usual. But I'm *terribly* afraid you'll have to clear your desk as soon as possible.'

'I know. Like Rodge and Chloë.'

'This evening,' said Sacker quietly. 'If you can.'

'It's all right,' said Terry. 'I haven't got much to take.'

There didn't seem to be anything to say after that, and Terry rose from his chair in the awkward silence. Sacker smiled the small, sad smile of a well-trained undertaker, and Terry reflected it back at him before walking out into the main office. At his desk, he realised quite how true his own last words had been; he'd laid no personal stamp on his workspace, and it was as bare and impersonal as if he'd been gone for a month already. He'd touched this place not at all, he thought, and, no matter how it had seemed at the time, it hadn't touched him either.

He switched off his computer for the last time and put on his coat. There was nobody to say goodbye to; the solitary copywriter had left while he'd been with Sacker, who was still in his office. Bright white striplights buzzed as he passed empty desks and dead black computer screens, bypassed the darkened kitchen and headed for the lifts.

There was no poignancy in leaving the building: it felt as disposable and impersonal as a paper cup. The only evocative thing was the night beyond. He felt its aching resonance more than ever as he walked – the bright lights, the icy darkness, the anonymous people. It hurt him with something beyond pain, and moved him.

For a fleeting second, he thought of returning to the club, but knew at once that he wouldn't. He'd have all of Rosina that he wanted soon. There were only two days left.

22

When Marie walked into the restaurant, Robert was sitting at a table by the window, waiting for her. The sight touched her deep inside with reassurance – a world a million miles away from Terry, and the tense silences in the kitchen. She hurried towards him.

'Hi,' she said, slightly awkwardly, sitting down, 'am I late?'

'No. I'm early,' he said, and smiled. 'What would you like to drink?'

'A glass of white wine, please.'

He summoned a passing waiter, and her drink arrived quickly. 'Well, cheers,' he said. They clicked their glasses, and sipped. Between them, a tall candle burned and an intense, ambiguous silence fell. She couldn't think how to break it. Quiet jazz music played in the background, behind other people's conversations, eloquent without words.

'So,' he said eventually. 'Get up to anything last weekend?'

'Had my niece round.' Suddenly she needed to mention her fears – it was almost a physical impulse, an urge to share them with someone who might understand. She backed away from it quickly, alarmed that it had ever been there. 'Nothing much else, really.'

'You don't have kids of your own?'

'No. He can't have kids, my husband. And he's never been keen on adopting.' Terry's eyes filled her mind and she struggled to speak without fear. 'It doesn't bother me, mind you. I never wanted a family much.'

'Me neither,' he said. 'My ex-wife did, I think. We never really had anything in common.'

She didn't want to speak as she did, but couldn't help herself: the clockspring tension inside her demanded release. 'Just like me and Terry. I wish I'd never married him sometimes, Robert. Swear to God.'

His eyebrows rose. 'Things not going well?'

'You could say that.' She spoke deliberately, without self-pity. 'We hardly speak to each other, these days.' She stopped before she was tempted to mention the darker problems – the things that didn't belong at a window table covered by a crisp white cloth, with candlelight glinting off the rim of a wine-glass, and soft music in the background.

'That's a shame,' he said. The waiter came to ask if they were ready, and they glanced over the menus, then ordered. When the man had gone, Robert leaned closer to her and spoke confidentially: 'You deserve better than a marriage like that.'

She was flattered, longing, aghast. 'Well,' she said, 'thanks.'

'I mean it, you know,' he said. 'I really mean it.' He sat across the table and watched her, with an expression that looked almost like sadness.

The food, when it arrived, was delicious, but Marie couldn't do it justice – she felt sick with uncertainty, and the prospect of going back. She wished she could stay here all night, where there was nothing to be afraid of, nothing that couldn't be named.

'Well,' she said finally, laying down her knife and fork, 'that was delicious,' and hoped he wouldn't comment on the fact that she'd barely touched it.

He didn't. 'Do you want a pudding?' he asked, his eyes not leaving hers.

'No, thanks,' she said. 'I'd better be getting home soon. It's almost nine.'

'Listen,' he said abruptly, 'how about I give you my home number? You've got my e-mail address already. Next time you want to come out, just call me or drop me a line. We'll sort something out.'

'Good idea,' she said. 'I'd give you *my* home number but . . .' And an image of Terry rose between them, vague and blurred to Robert, but to her, all too clear.

He got out his business card and wrote quickly on the back before handing it to her – she saw he'd put down both his home and mobile numbers. 'Do call, won't you?'

'I will,' she said quietly. 'You know I will.'

After he'd paid the bill, he offered again to drive her home, but she demurred with a kind of panic – she couldn't bear the two areas of her life to meet, to see Robert's profile silhouetted against the streets and landmarks that heralded fear. 'Well,' she said, outside the restaurant, 'I suppose I'll see you tomorrow.'

'Have a nice evening,' he said, and kissed her briefly on the lips – a quick, chaste kiss that said it all.

Marie got the tube to Brixton, then waited in the bus-stop crowd for some time. Finally, a bus drew up. She squeezed on as standing-room-only, feeling the hot cramped irritability around her as a kind of background music. Like the jazz in the restaurant, she thought, and felt the poignancy of her situation more deeply than ever – going back to a husband who'd become a stranger, leaving the comfort of Robert far behind.

She got off at her stop and began the walk home. As she reached the house, she saw that the living-room curtains were drawn and a thin streak of light showed between them – the frosted window above the front door was gold-lit and welcoming. Terry was home early for once, she thought.

She kept thinking about mentioning separation again, and couldn't understand why it seemed so difficult. She told herself she'd resurrect the issue tomorrow night.

Then she was walking down the path, and her key was turning in the front door.

23

'Sorry I'm late, love,' said Marie, hanging her coat up in the hallway. 'Had to stay late at work. You know how it is sometimes.'

'Tell me about it.' His imminent escape warmed and calmed him – his voice was easy, affectionate. 'Good day?'

As she came into the kitchen, she looked at him with faint

wariness. 'Not bad. Just the usual, really,' she said. Then, taking in the cooking smells and the table laid for two, 'You put the dinner on?'

'I thought I should.' And he had, and was amazed to find himself saying something to her that wasn't a lie. He could almost forget about the anger and the hatred in these last days, as long as they weren't triggered off by something beyond him. He could almost lose the darker things in recollected contentment. With salvation almost close enough to touch, he could remember the old days without bitterness. 'Sorry I've been back so late recently, Marie. I won't have to do it any more.'

'The busy time's tailed off?'

'Not exactly. But the creative director's got some new people in to handle the extra work. It's all going fine there, now. Really fine.'

'It seems it.' Something was dawning behind the surprise in her eyes. Terry thought it might be relief. 'You seem happier tonight.'

'Yeah,' he said. 'I am. I know I've been a bit off lately but I've been under a lot of pressure.'

Had he really thought of taking the butcher's knife from the cutlery drawer last Sunday, he wondered. That morning seemed miles away, years away. Now that the shore was in sight, the chances of being swept away had diminished. He wasn't on solid ground yet, but still, he felt safe. 'It should be ready now,' he said, rising from his seat. 'The dinner.'

'It's all right, love,' said Marie quickly, 'you sit down. I'll do it.'

She dished up the steak and kidney pie, the peas and new potatoes, laid his plate down, then hers and sat. They started to eat. 'So what have you been working on today?' she asked at last.

'Oh, you know. Just this and that.'

'Still Homebase?'

'Yeah,' he said, 'and some other stuff,' and he saw the night as a thin black strip through the almost-drawn blinds. The kitchen was bright and warm and comfortable, and the silence that gathered around them felt almost like contentment.

But it's not real contentment, Terry, the little voice whispered urgently, out of nowhere. *It only feels that way because you're lying to her, and to yourself. If she said one wrong thing to you, it might be one wrong thing too many – it might tip you over the edge all over again. Because you're not safe yet, Terry. And don't make the mistake of thinking you are—*

It smashed through the poignant peace of his penultimate evening at home like a brick through a window. He tried to push it away, but it was too late, the damage had been done. After dinner, Marie sat on the sofa beside him, and smiled at him almost like she'd used to, but it wasn't the same now. Suddenly he was aware that he was acting, and felt cold and tense inside. The little voice had been right, as it always was. The only real safety would come when he was far away from this woman, this house, this city. He was a danger still, and a far worse danger if he let himself forget it.

In bed that night, the dream drove home the message, and he woke up shaking, alert, sweating cold fear in the dark. He lay back on the pillow, and tried to soothe himself with three simple words. *One day left. One day left.*

24

On Thursday morning, he got up at the usual time, showered, shaved and dressed. Force of habit was so strong that it was only on his way downstairs that he remembered he had no work to go to, that he'd leave the house as he always did and then have the day to himself. It wasn't surprising, he thought, that it took him by surprise. During the week, showering, shaving and dressing had always been followed by work – it had been that way for as long as he could remember, for a hundred years.

But that had changed now, as everything had changed, and when he escaped with Rosina, the things that used to be wouldn't matter.

In the kitchen, the lights were on against the dark morning. Marie stood by the cooker. 'Morning, love,' she said, turning, smiling.

It was ironic, he thought, that she seemed to have regained at least some of her old trust in him when he was closer to the edge than he'd ever been. He smiled back at her, a look that said maybe they should try to start again. 'Morning, Marie,' he said. He sat down at the table, and she gave him his coffee. 'Thanks.'

Wind-driven rain rattled at the glass. Marie shivered. 'It's pouring out there,' she said. 'It's been horrible, the weather, lately.'

'I know.' He drank his coffee in silence. 'I'd better go, anyway,' he said. 'I'll be late for work.' Then he was putting on his coat, walking out into the shadowy morning, putting up his umbrella as he began his last day of uncertainty.

It felt indescribably strange, not having to go to the office in Soho Square. He didn't know where to go instead, then remembered he had some important business to attend to. Ingrained habit led him via the usual route into Oxford Street, where he bought a second coffee in Starbucks and drank it by the window. He looked out at wet grey streets, and faceless people scurrying past under a forest of umbrellas, and the NatWest bank across the road. He waited for nine thirty to come, for it to open.

When it did, he was the first person to approach the cashiers' windows. A fat spotty girl in her late teens looked at him with tired uninterest. 'Can I help you, sir?'

'I hope so,' he said. 'I've got a savings account here and I'd like to close it tomorrow. I want to withdraw the funds in cash.'

'Have you got your account details with you?'

'Yeah.'

He passed under the grille the card Marie didn't know

about. She took it, studied it, and tapped at her computer. He couldn't see what it said on the screen, but the five-figure number he'd read so often was clearly reflected in her astonishment. 'In cash?'

'Yes.' His voice trembled slightly. 'What's the problem?'

'I'm sorry, sir,' she said, 'I just have to go and check with my supervisor,' and then he was watching her hurrying away through the dividing glass.

It seemed to Terry that he spent hours at that window – his tension stretched out like elastic, further and further each second. It had to be this way, he thought, a symbolic severance of his last link with this world, folded fifties in a suitcase leaving no remaining channels by which he could be traced. A suitcase full of notes would feel like finality. Like freedom.

But what if they don't have that much in the bank, Terry? the little voice enquired. *What if you should have given them more notice?* And then a crisp-shirted middle-aged woman was walking over to the cashier's window, and there was no time left for apprehension.

'Can I see some identification, please, sir?'

He'd brought his passport with him, and passed it under the grille. She studied it, scribbled something on a form in front of her, pressed buttons as the girl had minutes before. He fought to stay calm and seem confident, but the endless silence forced speech like a thumbscrew. 'What's the problem?'

'No problem.' The keyboard-tapping stopped abruptly. She looked at him through the glass, serious, confidential. 'It's a lot of money to withdraw in cash, sir. I wouldn't carry that much round Oxford Street myself.'

Impossible to explain to this stranger that there was no other way, now, that burning the bridge that led home had become his only possible course of action. He spoke quietly and politely: 'That's my problem.'

'Of course, sir. What time would you like to come in and collect it?'

'About half twelve,' he said, 'tomorrow afternoon. I'll bring a briefcase for you to put it in.'

'That's fine, sir. I'll let the desk staff know so you won't have to queue. Just go up to the Enquiries desk and . . .' He barely took in the rest of their brisk exchange.

Outside, the tide of commuters had drained away, and Oxford Street was relatively quiet. From this point on, he had nothing to do. The day was his, to do whatever he liked with.

He walked for some time to Leicester Square, amazed by how desolate everything was outside the rush-hour. Even when he'd arrived in the heart of crowds and life, he found nothing but little groups of forlorn, bedraggled tourists, and a handful of pavement artists under faded umbrellas, and hard, steady rain that showed no sign of abating. He walked aimlessly until the knowledge that he had only one day left in this city began to gnaw queasily in his guts. He went into a cinema, only to find as the film began that he couldn't concentrate on it. In the warm, near-deserted darkness, before the vast, luminous screen, he sat lost in shadows, and thought about the near future, and Rosina, and the glorious prospect of salvation. And her cruel, childish laughter filled his mind, and it seemed that he could hear it even over the deafening surround-sound of a car chase.

That night would be the last he'd ever spend with Marie. He thought that he should do something to mark it out as special. No matter what the little voice told him, there was nothing to be afraid of with her now – a twisted romance twined round the coming evening, their last supper, he thought, an echo of the old days. Long ago after the awards ceremony when he'd come home with the statuette and the champagne, the world had looked beautiful, and the future had extended before them like a warm, fresh summer day. Sitting in a half-empty cinema with the world crashing around him, he remembered that night very clearly, a time when there had been nothing to escape from. She'd shrieked and laughed and cuddled and she'd loved him. She'd loved him.

He wanted to go back to that time too badly.

If only for one last night.

25

Marie turned down a side-road and kept walking. Although it was only six o'clock, the winter evening was dark as midnight, and the empty streets shone yellow-black under the street-lights. Now she was alone, the confusion that had nibbled at the back of her mind all day crept out into the foreground and took over. Certainties blurred and faded to a point where she couldn't be sure of anything.

Was the terrible time over? Could she and Terry really go back to the way things used to be?

Three days ago, the answer to that last question would have been a flat, straightforward no. It had seemed then that nothing could ever obliterate her memory of that long day spent thinking he'd killed himself, her terror when she'd turned from the photograph album and seen him standing in the study doorway. The night when she'd lain in bed and felt him watching her. But suddenly, in the light of the previous evening, everything seemed different. It was easy to believe that maybe things would be all right now, that he'd been telling her the truth after all.

Because of work, he'd said. *I've been under a lot of pressure at work.*

And while part of her knew it couldn't possibly be so simple, another part – the part that had always wanted to believe in happy endings – told her equally strongly that it could be, and was. That her fears had been ridiculous, and that there'd never been anything at home to fear.

We could still have a future together, she thought. Then, *But what about Robert?*

In the kitchen, she put the dinner on and waited for Terry to come home. At half-past seven, she heard him let himself in. 'Hello Terry—' she began, then turning, seeing the bottle of champagne under his arm, she took a small step back. '*Well.* What's the occasion?'

'No occasion.' He smiled his old smile, handed her the bottle, hung up his wet coat in the hallway. 'I just thought it'd be nice, that's all.'

'Well,' she said again – bewildered, delighted. 'How lovely. Suppose we'd better put it in the fridge for a bit.' He nodded and laughed. He seemed even happier than he had last night, she thought, reckless but not unsettlingly so – as if he was celebrating some once-in-a-lifetime occasion, as if he was about to go on holiday. 'We can have it after dinner,' he said, and he sat down at the table, and she served up the meal.

When they'd finished, he offered to wash up, but she wouldn't let him. Suddenly, she felt guilty for what she'd said and thought about him while she was with Robert, and felt as if she had to make amends to him in some small symbolic way. Alone in the kitchen, she listened to the television through the half-open living-room door, and experienced a contentment she hadn't felt here in a very long time. He wasn't a bad husband, she thought, as she scrubbed at a plate. Maybe they still had a future together – anything was possible if he'd gone back to being the man she'd loved, the man she'd married.

She finished the washing-up, got the champagne out of the fridge, brought it into the living-room along with two glasses. 'Do you want to open it, or shall I?'

'It's all right. I will.' He got up, opened the bottle at the sideboard – the cork popped with a satisfying fizz – and poured. 'Well,' he said, handing her a glass, 'cheers.'

Cheers, said Robert in her mind – she hurried away from the memory. She didn't know what to think about Robert any more, didn't want his image confusing the unexpected joy of this evening. 'Cheers,' she echoed, and they drank.

They sat together just like they'd used to, and watched TV for some time. There was a recent film on BBC2 at half past eight, and they changed channels for it. When the end credits started rolling, it was nearly twenty to eleven. 'Have another glass,' he said. 'There's still almost half the bottle left.'

He reached over to top up her glass. In the lamplight, the

champagne looked like molten gold, and she remembered the night he'd won the award more vividly than ever. 'I'll get drunk,' she said, giggling, but she drank anyway, and he drank with her, and the bleakness of the night outside was forgotten.

'Do you ever wonder what it would have been like,' he asked unexpectedly, 'if we could have had a son together?'

'Not really. It never seemed that important.' She watched him, startled – his eyes were wistful and reflective. 'Why d'you ask?'

'I don't know. I just wondered. It doesn't matter now.' His reckless good humour returned, and he topped up their glasses again, and they finished the bottle between them.

In bed that night, they made love for the first time in a long time, and it was as good as it had ever been between them. She found him hungry in a way he'd never been before, but there was nothing perfunctory or clumsy in his urgency. The talcum-scented, familiar darkness became erotic as it had never been, and it lasted for ever, and not long enough.

Once, she hadn't slept for fear, but tonight, tentative happiness blocked out exhaustion. She lay in his arms and felt the slow rise and fall of his chest against her bare skin. The small unconscious smile on his lips moved her with intense tenderness, and the sense of his remote, peaceful dream lulled her into vague dreams of her own.

26

The following morning, Terry seemed even more ebullient, happy, and restless as a child on Christmas Eve. 'There you go, love,' she said, setting his coffee in front of him. 'Looking forward to work today, it seems.'

'Yeah,' he said. 'There's a big new pitch coming up. I'll be working on it later.'

'Well, stay as late as you have to.' She was astonished at how natural it felt now to say that. 'Honestly. I don't mind.'

'I won't have to.' He finished his coffee and stood up. 'Well,' he said, 'suppose I'd better get going.' And before he left the house, he kissed her, a long, slow, leisurely kiss that felt as if they had all the time in the world, and none at all.

When he'd gone, she brushed her hair, put on a little makeup and left for work. As she got out of the lift and her office came into view, she realised that within two short days her reaction to it had changed. It didn't look like sanctuary any more, just an inevitable continuation of the day – a place that would never be as pleasant as home. She couldn't have said how she felt about Robert now, and couldn't bear to admit to herself that she still found him attractive. Not now she felt happy in her marriage again.

It can't have sorted itself out just like that, she thought, and you know that deep down. You're not dumb enough to believe in a miracle. But she flinched away from the thought, not wanting to hear its stark truth. Because the nightmare time was over, wasn't it? Everything was fine?

At lunch-time, she walked to the sandwich shop on her own. Cheryl and Sandra were standing in the queue, chatting, and they greeted her as she came in. When they'd been served, they stood by the drinks cabinet and waited for her. 'All right, Marie?' asked Cheryl, as she joined them.

'Yeah.' It amazed her to realise that it wasn't a lie. 'I'm fine.'

They walked together back to the office. It had just stopped raining. The afternoon was grey and overcast, but festive lights sparkled with bright primary colours in shop windows, restaurants and cafés. 'Christmas is getting closer,' said Sandra. 'Be here in no time.'

'You doing anything much over the season?' Cheryl asked Marie.

'Me and Terry might go abroad.' It was the first time she'd thought about it for months, but she found it both plausible and alluring. 'We talked about it this summer, but didn't think we'd be able to afford it.'

'But now you can?'

'Yeah. Maybe we'll go to Greece or somewhere. It'd make a nice change,' said Marie. 'I'm sure Mum and Dad could do without us for once.'

'That's a good idea,' said Sandra. 'A Christmas to remember.'

'Yeah,' said Marie, and realised that she was actually looking forward to going home and sharing the idea with Terry. No matter what that nagging inner voice told her, things *had* gone back to the way they used to be. She walked beside Cheryl and Sandra through the commercial Christmas lights, knowing there was nothing left to fear in the world.

27

Terry walked out of NatWest with a battered black leather briefcase in one hand. He'd brought it from home that morning, leaving it in the hallway alcove on his way into the kitchen, sneaking it out as he left so Marie wouldn't see it. Now it contained the money his father had left him three months ago, the five-figure sum he'd stared at and dreamed of for so long. It occurred to him that his future and his freedom could be grabbed at any second by an opportunistic street thief, and he gripped the handle a little tighter.

Down Oxford Street he walked, and was overcome by the finality of it all. He'd got used to thinking in terms of days, but now he was living his last hours here – everywhere he looked he saw something he'd never see again. He'd never see Marie again or Lisa. And the force of his relief was immeasurable. Because he was safe now. Everything was safe.

He got the tube to Victoria, and the train to Streatham Hill from there. It seemed no time at all till home was in sight – home that wouldn't be home soon – and his key was turning in the front door. Then it swung shut behind him, and he started up the stairs.

In the bedroom, he laid the briefcase on the bed and opened it. Taped and folded rolls of notes looked back at him, thrilled and soothed him. It wasn't just a number on a screen, it was real now, and always had been. He gazed at it, fascinated, until he pulled himself together and slammed the briefcase. He took down his rarely used suitcase from the top of the wardrobe, and quickly packed what belongings he thought he'd need in a future spent far from here. He didn't know why he hurried – Marie would be out all day – but somehow he felt as if he had to. A new urgency filled him.

Downstairs, he set down the briefcase and suitcase in the hallway. He tore off a sheet from the telephone pad and picked up the pen that rested beside it. 'Remember Katie? It's not going to happen again. I won't let it,' he scrawled. 'This is the best way. I'm sorry. Terry.' He looked down at the words he'd just written, and the sight of them drove home the reality of today as nothing else had, and he was terrified, exhilarated, elated by the prospect of freedom.

Freedom and Rosina, he thought. He laid the note on the kitchen table, and walked back out in the hallway, where his cases were.

How strange it felt, to pick up his briefcase and suitcase in a place he knew so well, knowing that he'd never be there again. He looked around him with a stranger's eyes – at the closed door that led on to the study, the half-open living-room door showing a thin slice of sofa, the kitchen that had formed the backdrop to a terrible dream he'd never have again. He took a long, deep, shuddering breath, opened the front door and stepped out into the future.

Although it was only half past one and he had nothing to do for the rest of the day, he couldn't go to Rosina's flat now. It seemed important that he only went there that night, as they'd agreed – theirs was a relationship based on ritual, created around the uneasy rules of the club. When they were alone together, it would all be different but for now it was the same, and endless hours of waiting stretched out before him. In a quiet pub, he sat down at a corner table and ordered lunch. When it arrived, he realised, without surprise, that he had no appetite.

Her recollected laughter echoed in his mind, background music to disparate images. He remembered bright shards of light from the disco globe spinning idly across the Delilah's dance-floor, and was full of an almost intolerable longing.

The little voice said, *It's almost time, Terry...*

28

I'm scared, Rosina, Christine had said, in her pathetic, whining way, long ago. *I'm scared, Rosina.*

Christ, how she'd *hated* her.

Rosina lay in a bath that smelt of the Escape perfume which had coloured the white-and-pinewood bedroom in Chelsea, preparing herself for the time ahead. He'd be round in a few hours' time. She'd already packed. *I want to escape with you,* he'd said, *for ever,* and the memory of his earnest voice made her smile.

So silly, she thought, and pulled out the plug. She rose, naked, from the bath and padded into the black-walled room that always smelt of the bubbles she'd just bathed in. She wondered what to wear. She couldn't wear a dress tonight, she thought. It would seem wrong, somehow. Out of place.

But she would wear black. She always wore black. Because stupid little Christine hadn't liked black, and stupid little Christine's likes and dislikes now provided an inverse barometer to her own.

She sat down at her dressing-table, still naked, and began to brush her hair. Her black-haired, cold-eyed reflection stared back at her. She remembered how Christine had looked in mirrors – overawed, babyish, naïve – and the sense of mingled loathing and triumph was beyond the world.

She laid down the hairbrush and walked over to the wardrobe. She remembered the wardrobe in Chelsea. It had been beautiful, as everything had been there: the photographs and the garden and Leo and Annabel Parker. In a way, she supposed, it had created the woman she was now. It had taught her how to hate and how to love. It had taught her everything she'd ever know about the nature of power.

A quiet, lonely teenage bedroom. A baby crying in a pram. Stupid little Christine silenced for ever.

An underground hostess bar called Delilah's—

'Rosina,' Terry had groaned into her neck, and it excited her just to think of it, because while he thought he knew about Christine, he didn't know a thing – didn't know why she kept the locked wooden box on her dressing-table, or what it contained.

But there was no point in thinking about Christine now. He'd be round in a couple of hours. Rosina selected an outfit and put it on. Then sat down on the bed, a black-haired girl in a black-walled room that always smelt of Escape, and the past.

29

Marie got off the bus at her stop, and walked home quickly. In the windows all the lights were off. Terry should be home soon, she thought – she didn't expect he'd be staying late tonight. She got out her key and let herself in.

She hung her coat in the hallway, stepped into the kitchen and switched on the lights – flattering rosy-gold illuminated familiar empty silence, and something that jarred. A folded note on the otherwise bare kitchen table – a name in handwriting she recognised at once.

'Marie,' she read, as she picked it up, and she noticed the

oddity of the address – who else was going to pick up a note left in here? – before she unfolded it and started reading.

'God,' she said quietly. 'Oh, my God.'

In the grip of a kind of shell-shock, she walked slowly up to the bedroom they shared. The suitcase he always kept on top of the wardrobe was gone. She opened the wardrobe doors, and saw that most of his clothes were, too.

She sat down heavily on the double bed. *This can't be happening,* she thought. *This has to be a bad dream.* But she knew deep inside that it could, and it wasn't. This was reality, and he'd gone.

She looked back to the night before, and understood what the champagne had meant, the affection in the living room, the final urgent passion in the bed she sat on now. Of course he'd made it special. He'd understood what she hadn't – that it had been the last evening they'd ever spend together.

And the first name to come into her mind wasn't Sandra, or Mum, or even Allie. It was Robert.

Downstairs, in the hallway, she got out her wallet and extracted the card he'd given her. She carried it to the telephone in a hand that shook slightly. His small neat writing was as easy to decipher as type. She pressed out his mobile number with the receiver gripped tight against her ear, and waited.

He answered on the fifth ring. 'Hello?'

'Robert, it's Marie.'

'Marie! How are you?'

'Not good. You're not going to believe what's happened.' She broke off for a second, taking a long, deep, shuddering breath. 'My husband's left me. He's just – *run away*—'

Her voice splintered into tears that she couldn't hold back. He let her cry for a moment, then spoke again, quiet and reassuring. 'What happened?'

'He left a note. Such a strange note. It frightens me. He's taken his clothes. Nearly all his clothes.' Her voice was weak and shaking, almost inaudible. 'My God, Robert, what am I going to do?'

'Give me your address. I'll be right over.'

She told him, could hear tiny scratching noises as he wrote it down. 'The nearest railway station's Streatham Hill,' she said. 'We're just off the main road from there. Thirteen Addington Road. First on the right.'

'I'm on my way,' he said. 'I'll be round in an hour or so.'

'Thanks, Robert,' she said numbly, and the phone went down in her ear.

She hung up with slow, uncertain movements, went into the living room and sat down. The words Terry had written echoed in her mind. *Remember Katie? That's not going to happen again. I won't let it.* Deep inside, she tried to pretend that she couldn't understand their potential significance. She waited for Robert to arrive.

30

Terry had stayed in the pub all afternoon and evening, reading a newspaper someone had left behind at the next table. The same flat, lifeless words unwound before him, over and over again. His restlessness had grown, minute by minute, hour by hour, to become as unbearable as cramp. At first he'd drunk orange juice, but as the afternoon had turned into night, he'd switched to pints. He sat at the corner table with the future burning a hole in his mind, listening to the mundane sounds of a pub getting busy in the early evening, thinking of champagne in metal buckets, the beauty and the languor of drifting disco lights.

Now he checked his watch, and saw that it was eight o'clock. It was time.

This is it, he thought. He set down his glass, rose from the table and picked up his cases. As he walked out into the rainy darkness, the excitement he felt was almost nauseating – like the last few seconds before you puked into the slipstream of a cheap fairground ride, like the dizzying beginning of the end.

His life here was over and he was safe at last.

But it doesn't feel like you thought it would, does it, Terry? Not quite.

The tube led him to Earl's Court station on the District line. Crowded, ramshackle and dingy, it brought a cold breath of obscure 1930s movies, and he felt as if he'd wandered on to the wrong film set by mistake. Try as he might to recapture his earlier euphoria, it simply refused to come. He felt lost and afraid, full of new doubts that murmured at the back of his mind. He sat down on a bench, got out the card with her address, unfolded it and read it through.

'Turn right out of the station,' she'd written, '91 Hillcrest Road, ring the bell for Flat 6.'

The neatness of her handwriting had surprised him when he'd first seen it in the club, but realised at once that his surprise was ridiculous – there was nothing untidy about her: her every word and gesture expressed an offhand precision. Suddenly, however, he saw that there was something strange about its neat loops and round, closed letters – something that struck a discordant note in the shadows of this grimy station. Something that was far too effortful.

He rose quickly from the bench and picked up his briefcase and suitcase. He had to see her again for himself: the beauty and the mystery and the nameless quality that had enraptured him from the start. He would feel better when he saw her. He walked out of the station and turned right.

31

Marie sat on the sofa in the living room and listened to the kettle boiling in the kitchen. Robert had arrived maybe five minutes ago. She'd offered to make him a cup of tea, but on seeing her white face and haunted eyes, he'd persuaded her to sit down, insisted on making it himself.

He came out of the kitchen with a mug in his hand, gently transferred it into hers. Although the room was centrally heated, as the rest of the house was, she was freezing cold, and gripped the warm china like a hot-water bottle for comfort.

'Thanks, Robert,' she said.

'It's okay. I know it's a stupid thing to say but try and calm down.'

They sat for a while without speaking. 'I just don't know what to do,' she said at last. 'The note he left didn't make sense.'

'Is it private?' he asked. 'Or can I see it?'

She had it beside her on the arm of the sofa, passed it to him, then watched him read it. After a minute or so, he spoke. 'Who's Katie?'

'She was his little sister. She died when he was ten.'

There was a sharp new note to his voice. 'What happened to her?'

'She was murdered. Strangled.'

They looked at each other. The suspicion had been somewhere in her mind ever since she'd first read the note, but she'd forced it away. 'No,' she said quietly. 'He couldn't have. It's *impossible*.' But Robert just sat and looked at her, and didn't say a word.

32

The last few streets unwound rapidly. Friday-night crowds of teenagers and twentysomethings roamed under the street-lights, and Terry walked alone. An endless succession of noises echoed in his ears and meant nothing – a girl's jagged, hysterical laughter, a squeal of brakes, a man shouting. As he walked past closed shops and open pubs, restaurants and newsagents he'd never seen before, Terry felt the only world he'd ever known falling away around him, leaving nothing but a deeper and more final truth he couldn't yet see. And the only remaining certainty was that a black-haired girl would be waiting for him, and he clung to the knowledge as though it were a lifebelt, and hid from his new fears in wild thoughts of the future.

We'll be together, he thought, and I'll be safe, and then Hillcrest Road came in sight and he was almost there.

He turned down the road. The houses he passed were tall, white and shabby. Even in the half-light of the streetlamps, peeling paint and overflowing dustbins showed up clearly, at once seedy and evocative. He followed the street numbers. At number ninety-one something caught in his throat, and he tasted the dizzying joy of escape all over again – rosy light filtering mistily through dirty net curtains, a sordid yet somehow glorious nemesis that had always been lying in wait for his footsteps.

You're here now, Terry.

His fears left him. He walked up to the tall front door and stood looking at the house for a few seconds. He steeled himself, pressed the doorbell that said 'Flat 6' and waited.

Then the front door creaked open, and she was there.

33

She looked different.

She stood in front of an ugly, dark-carpeted hallway, wearing tight black trousers, tight black T-shirt, high-heeled black boots. Under a tired yellow overhead light, her red lipstick looked somehow too heavy, too brassy. Not theatrical. Cheap.

'Hello,' she said.

'Well – I'm here.' He stepped in and closed the door behind him, trying to calm his fears with a recklessness to match her own. 'I'm ready.'

'Good,' she said. 'Now we can *escape together.*'

Was it his imagination, or was there something different in the timbre of her voice? Smooth, he'd thought it, melodious, but now he detected a hard metallic edge behind the surface drawl. 'I suppose I'd better make you a drink or something,' she said. 'Before we go.'

'What have you got?'

'Vodka,' she said. 'Just follow me.'

He walked up the steep narrow staircase behind her. Watching her back, he thought suddenly that the colour of her hair was all wrong. You said black hair when you meant dark hair, but hers was the same shade as her T-shirt – flat, one-dimensional, unreal. Dyed.

'Here we are,' she said, turning a doorhandle. 'Home sweet home.'

He stepped into a large bed-sitting room with the walls painted a mottled, patchy black, a messy kitchenette in an alcove, a closed door that could only lead on to the bathroom. Everything he saw was both shabby and prosaic – an old dark-wood dressing-table with a silver crack running through the mirror-glass, a scarlet chiffon scarf tossed over an unshaded lamp, turning the room an ugly, ominous red. Only the perfume on the air was expensive, and its subtle notes didn't belong here. It smelt like a cool, sweet breath from another world.

'This your room?'

'No,' she said, 'the Pope's,' but her indifference seemed brittle and false in a way it never had before, and her laughter would have been at home in any pub or launderette. It was just as it had always been, but now it had become harsh and artificial and somehow desperate, and the sound chilled his soul.

'It's not what I'd have thought,' he said. 'Not at all.'

'Well. You live and learn.' She raised a hand to brush her too-black hair out of her eyes. He saw that her dark nail-varnish was chipped round the edges. 'Sit down. I'll get your drink.'

She walked over to the dressing-table by the wide, low bed. A bottle of vodka with maybe two inches left stood beside a plastic bottle of Diet Coke, near a jumbled heap of makeup. She had her back to him as she poured, and he saw her reflected in the cracked mirror. The light in here hurt his eyes – dark, garish, unsettling.

'I took out my savings,' he said. 'All the money my father left me. It's for us.'

'What do you mean?' she asked absently, trying to unscrew the bottle of Coke.

'What do you think?' He unfastened the briefcase and set it on the bed. Fifty-pound notes stared out in thick bundles, real and undeniable. 'We're going to need something to live on.'

'Oh, of course,' she said, and her laughter was more terrible than ever. 'The fucking lid's stuck on this thing. I can't budge it.'

Frantically, he reached for the freedom of the darkness, the life without limits that he'd dreamed of for so long. 'I've run away from everything,' he said. 'And I'm never going back.'

'You're so silly.' She twisted at the lid through a handful of her T-shirt. 'You know you don't mean it.'

'We'll start a whole new life,' he said. 'Everything'll be different, from now on.'

'So where did you tell your wife you were going?' she asked. '*Really?*' And in that moment, he knew she'd never meant any of this – that her recklessness had been no more than ignorance of the truth, that she hadn't believed he'd run away from everything in his life and never go back to it, and had treated the only dream he'd ever have now as a kind of far-fetched joke. A tidal wave of horror overcame him, and he slammed the briefcase a split second before the bottle hissed and fizzed and opened, and Rosina turned round.

34

'What have you got in there?' she asked, when she saw his hand lying protectively on top of it.

'Nothing. Just some things from the office.'

She poured sparingly, frowning over the contents of his glass. 'There's not much vodka left,' she said, handing it to him. 'I thought there was.'

Red glinting up at him from his drink, gleaming in her pale-blue eyes. His sense of nightmare was indescribable. 'I'll go and buy some,' he said, wanting more than anything to get away from her. 'I passed a shop on the way here.'

'It's all right. You stay here. I'll go.' She set the bottles back on the dressing-table, walked over to the wardrobe and got out a black leather jacket. 'Are we going on holiday tonight or what?' she asked, slipping it on. 'Where are we staying?'

For a second, he looked at her and saw her as she really was: shabby, unstable, lost as he was. 'Don't worry,' he heard himself say cheerfully, 'it's a secret.'

'Well, I'll get the vodka,' she said. 'I won't be ten minutes. Make yourself at home.'

He didn't watch her leave. He couldn't bear to. He fixed his gaze somewhere in the middle distance, hearing the door closing and her footsteps descending the stairs. The creak and slam of the heavy front door as she left. Someone in the next flatlet had their stereo on loud, muffled by the wall. It was playing a song he'd last heard in Delilah's: the hard disco beats pounded in his head like a migraine.

He sat on the bed and drained the contents of his glass in one. His heart pounded in his chest but the rest of him felt dead, numb. He might as well finish the bottle, he thought dispassionately – he might as well do anything, now. He walked over to the dressing-table and reached for the remains of the vodka, but his fingers felt like someone else's, as if he was operating them by remote control. As he reached, he knocked over a long, narrow wooden box with a brass fastening and a keyhole. It fell to the floor with a hard crash, and a snapping noise that said the lock had just popped open.

Almost unconsciously, he bent down to collect its contents – a photograph and a passport. He was in the process of replacing them when curiosity overcame him.

He picked up the photograph first and studied it. It showed the head and shoulders of a girl in neat school uniform. At first he thought it was Rosina, then realised it wasn't. The girl's features were more delicate, finer-drawn, and her eyes were the darkest he'd ever seen.

But there was something familiar about her all the same. Something about the way she looked out. Cold, assured, half amused. It was the same heartlessly compelling look that had hypnotised him in the drifting disco lights of Delilah's, on the narrow red-carpeted stairs. And he had the sudden feeling that if this girl could step out of the photograph and speak her cool drawling voice would hold no metallic edge, and her laughter would be the laughter he'd fallen in love with, amoral, fearless, cruel as the night.

He knelt on the fraying carpet that didn't quite reach the edges of the room, where ancient lino showed through, black and green. Music from next door muttered through the wall as he laid down the photograph and picked up the passport. In the gory light, he turned to the back of it, and stopped dead.

The photograph showed Rosina.

The name said *Christine Molloy.*

35

Of course, she was Christine on paper. Just as she always had been.

But that didn't matter any more. She'd made herself into what she'd always wanted to be, what she'd envied beyond words. A girl who'd drifted out of her life like a passing dream nine years ago, whose cold, corrupt, assured amorality she'd yearned to possess.

Rosina Parker, of Chelsea . . .

The girl who had taken her name walked in the darkness and the steadily deepening rain towards the shop. She thought about the man she was about to go away with, and experienced a bitter tenderness. He was, she thought, so much like she'd used to be – like part of her occasionally suspected she still was. Angry, bitter and trapped, seeking out something he'd never have in the thin, rosy lights of the club – anonymity, escape, a kind of salvation.

Desperately believing in something far from home.

He thought of her as Rosina, and in his mind it was more than just the false name that it was to the other girls at Delilah's, more than just a convenient concealing of identity. In his mind it was everything she'd ever wanted it to be – everything she'd dreamed of since her early teens.

She remembered how she'd felt back then, as Christine, when she'd seen her reflection beside that of the real Rosina. How she'd hated and despised herself for the things she didn't have and never would – how she yearned to be the girl she saw beside her. To have her confidence and her unselfconscious, childish laughter, her cruelty and her power to inspire adoration . . .

She had it all, now. When she was with Terry, she had it all. Because in the shadows of a Soho hostess bar, nobody ever knew who you really were, and you were free to become anything you wanted. It was why she'd started working there; it was why she'd stayed.

She'd changed the way she laughed, the way she spoke, the colour of her hair. All she hadn't been able to change was her handwriting. And she supposed it didn't matter all that much. She couldn't imitate Rosina Parker's careless, confident, elegant scrawl – but she rarely wrote anyway, these days. In the club.

I'm her, now, she thought, and a sense of triumph howled in her mind as the rain lashed down around her. *I've made myself into her.* Then the bright lights of the shop came into view, and she walked on to meet them.

36

We'll escape together, he'd said to her. *For ever.*

But the salvation he'd depended on wasn't going to happen after all, and the future of safety and happiness he'd seen had been no more than a mirage. Because there was no safety. And there was no future. And the girl he'd pinned his final dreams on had turned out to be nothing but a living, breathing lie.

If she wasn't Rosina, there was nothing left.

He stood by the bed in the shabby, black-walled room. His breath came slow and deep. The belt in his hands had come from a drawer she'd left half open. It was thin black leather with a heavy silver buckle. He remembered his dream of killing his sister and what he'd said to her in it – what, although he had no memory of the event, he must surely have said in the orchard.

Do you want to play a game, Katie?

And it hadn't really been Katie's fault, or old Harkness's fault, or even – really – Julia Fielding's fault, but it had been the black-haired girl's fault, and his last act in this world would be no more than simple justice. Because she'd lied to him. Because she'd *never been Rosina.*

The front door creaked open downstairs.

It's a good game, Katie, he'd said in the dream, and the cracked mirror showed him a pale set face in a light the colour of blood, and he held the belt just as he must have held the skipping-rope. *I'll show you how to play it—*

Footsteps moved up the stairs.

He stood with a belt in his hands and a new sense of peace in his mind as he prepared to kill her. He waited for the door across the room to open. In his mind, he felt the darkness coming down for the first time in twenty-seven years.

37

There was usually a queue in the shop, but tonight, Rosina saw, it was more daunting than ever, fully eight people long. She joined it, and waited.

She was looking forward to going on holiday, she thought, with Terry. It would be nice to have his fascinated adoration all to herself for maybe two weeks, somewhere far from this city, from the club. And, in his eyes, she'd be Rosina anywhere.

I am Rosina. These days, I am. *I got rid of Christine a long time ago, locked her away, or killed her, or both. So I don't have to be her any more. And who'd want to be pathetic little Christine when they could be Rosina?*

She remembered Christine's life – an ugly little terraced house, parents who only spoke to each other to argue, and only spoke to her to nag, criticise, or pressurise. Always the pressure to achieve. Had to get the As, then the scholarship, then keep her grades up. Had to do the right thing, the conventional thing, just so they could show her off to acquaintances and claim her achievements as their own. But they never congratulated her in private.

Sitting in the cramped respectable bedroom, hot tears running down her face as she listened to them argue downstairs and realised she'd have to do her homework for the morning. Thinking about phoning Rosina.

Want to be her. Everything would stop mattering, if I was her.

The fury when she and Rosina had been expelled. The humiliation of her mother's tears in the head's office. The pain of their harsh, uncaring hostility on the too-long drive home, and the certainty that she'd failed them. She wasn't their all-achieving only child any more, and they let her know it. In the days and weeks and months that followed, how they let her know it.

If I was Rosina, they wouldn't look at me like that. And even if they did, I wouldn't care a bit.

The helplessness when Rosina had stopped taking her calls. The half-formed ideas of suicide, leading on to another idea that stayed, and set, and hardened. The deepening conviction that she *could* move away from herself. In another place, another world, where she could be anything she wanted.

Rosina never had to achieve. Rosina never had to be anything but herself.

She was sixteen and a half when she left home. Her parents never tried to track her down. But the overwhelming guilt of having failed and disappointed them began to fade when she dyed her hair black in an anonymous bedsit, and when she looked at herself in the mirror, cold blue eyes looked back with a familiar mockery that thrilled her. In her mind, she saw a beautiful three-storey house in Chelsea. The world that had banished her.

That had banished *Christine.*

But Christine didn't exist any more. Not now.

Rosina stood in the too-long queue and felt her reverie fade around her. Suddenly, she realised she also had to buy nail-polish remover, because her nails were slightly chipped, and if she didn't do them tonight, Terry might notice. She left the queue and went to the back of the shop to pick up the little bottle. When she returned, the queue had grown by another three people. She stood, and sighed, and waited.

38

When the darkness lifted, Terry was standing alone in Rosina's room, just as he had been before. He had no idea how much time had passed. All he knew was that the footsteps on the stairs had moved on and away, and he had done nothing.

Then the little voice in his mind spoke up, and the quiet words held more authority than they ever had.

It's not her fault, Terry. No matter who she said she was.

But she lied to me!

And you lied to her. Did you tell her the truth about Katie, Terry? About that terrible dream?

Silence. Endless red-lit silence.

I thought you wanted to escape the violence, Terry. But now you're going back to it all over again. Is this the freedom you wanted so badly, Terry? Is this the safety you wanted?

His face in the cracked mirror. The haunted, hunted look in the pale eyes that watched him.

There's only one way you'll ever be free of it all, Terry. Because it's all in you, and always has been. And it'll stay with you as long as you live. Wherever you go and whoever you go with, you'll never escape. But there's a way out. A way to escape from the violence.

The voice spoke in his mind. He stood for long minutes, and listened.

When it had fallen silent, he let the belt drop, almost silently, to the floor. Then he walked out of the black-walled room, down the narrow stairs that stirred with strangers' music and out into the night.

39

The man behind the till handed Rosina her change without speaking. She picked up the carrier-bag and walked out of the shop, wishing suddenly that she'd brought her umbrella. The rain fell in solid sheets, plastering her hair to her scalp.

She turned down her street, and saw a figure hurrying across the road. For a second, she thought it was Terry, but it couldn't be: he was sitting in her room, waiting for her to return. In this light and this weather everyone looked much the same, and she quickened her pace. She let herself in to the building she lived in and hastened up the stairs, towards a man and a holiday and an adoration that she knew she wasn't entitled to, but wanted too badly anyway.

She opened the door to her room, and her breath froze in her throat.

For a too-brief second, she was sure he must be in the bathroom, but something in the quality of the silence told her that he wasn't, and she understood that she was alone. *It* was *him*, she thought wildly. *I saw him walking away.* Then she saw what was lying on the floor next to the chest of drawers, and moved over to the three items with the slow steps of a sleepwalker. Her passport. Her silver-buckled belt. Her only surviving photograph of Rosina Parker.

Slow horror blossomed in her mind. Then and there, she knew she'd never see him again, and understood exactly what had driven him away.

He knew about Christine. About her and Christine.

And she had no idea how he'd gleaned the whole story from a passport and a dog-eared photograph taken seven years ago, but that didn't matter, and she sat down on the bed in the red light and wept long, racking sobs that convulsed her whole body. Because there was no Terry now, and no holiday, no tentative adoration or power to corrupt. There was nothing left but the truth of herself. For now. For ever.

The perfume that Rosina had always worn filled her senses, made her cry even harder, and she leaned back on the bed to lie full-length. Her elbow struck a hard edge. She turned, her tears cut off mid-sob. How could she not have noticed that he'd left his suitcase – his briefcase?

He couldn't have *forgotten* them. They must have been staring him in the face.

Had he left them here on purpose?

Curiosity proved stronger than despair, after all. Perhaps because it was smaller and easier to lift, she reached first for the briefcase. It was old, shabby-looking, of scuffed black leather, and had no combination lock. She flicked back the brass fastenings that held it shut, and looked inside.

40

He knew he'd left his suitcase and briefcase in her room. It didn't matter. Once, he'd thought his father's legacy was important, but now he understood that it meant less than nothing. Because it couldn't save him, after all. Not now.

He walked through the night, not knowing where he was or where he was going, and rain lashed down around him. Images and words filled his mind – a sleazy hotel room, and a bleak office, and a too-bright classroom where he'd sat ignored, a sunny orchard and a ticking clock and a red-lit room that smelt of perfume. It had all been leading to this, he realised, from the start. And the world crumbled around him as he watched, leaving nothing but a freedom that was more terrible than anything he'd ever known.

Nothing left but the end now, Terry.

When he finally became aware of where he was, he was standing on Chelsea Bridge, soaked to the skin. A fast-flowing river of traffic moved behind him. The railing came up to chest height. He gripped it tightly and looked down into black, swirling water. There was oblivion in that sight. It called out to him.

Remember Julia, Terry?

The beauty of the drop.

Remember Katie, Terry?

Infinity unfolding beneath him.

Nowhere left to go, Terry, the little voice told him, and he pulled himself up by his hands, and jumped.

Epilogue

'Your sister's great,' said Robert.

They were driving back from Allie's flat in the close, sultry July evening. Marie turned in the passenger seat to smile at him. 'I'm glad you like her. Makes things easier.'

'Lisa's a sweet kid too.'

'I can't believe she's almost ten now. Where did all the time go?' A brief silence fell between them. 'I'm pleased for Allie, you know,' Marie said eventually. 'I never really thought she'd get a record deal.'

'Stands to reason she'd want to celebrate that,' said Robert. 'It was a good party.' And they drove for a while in silence before home came into sight – the four-bedroomed house in Hampstead into which they'd moved two years ago, when they'd married.

As Robert parked the car, Marie let herself in and switched on the lights. Alone in the kitchen, a vague melancholy that had haunted her all day became deeper, stronger, more poignant. It was exactly three years since the night of Terry's death – a morbid anniversary that she never marked, that Robert never seemed to remember, that Allie hadn't known about when she'd scheduled her record-deal party.

Did she miss him? She didn't know. She was happy with Robert, there was no question about it. But sometimes, privately, she couldn't help but dwell on the details of her first husband's mysterious suicide. Three years ago, at half past nine, the water of the Thames had been like ice, and Terry had been dead before the passer-by who'd seen him jump could summon help.

That was terrible enough. But what she'd found out a year later . . .

Then Robert was there, kissing her cheek, suggesting that they opened a bottle of wine and spent the rest of the evening on the patio.

Beyond the french windows that led out from the kitchen, they sat at the patio table, sipped from their glasses and watched each other. The dark garden extended endlessly beyond the floodlit stone patio, and little lights from other people's houses glinted like fireflies.

Marie took a deep breath. 'Do you ever think,' she asked abruptly, 'about the note Terry left?'

'Sometimes.' He sounded cautious, surprised. 'Why do you ask?'

'I've meant to tell you for a long time. It just never seemed the *right* time . . .'

'What?'

'Remember the April before last? Just before we got married? When I told you I was having trouble sleeping?' She saw the memory in his eyes, and carried on quickly. 'I kept thinking about him, Robert. Thinking he might have killed his sister and got away with it. I just couldn't stand the . . . not knowing. Started thinking I'd have to check it out. So I did.'

His eyebrows shot up. 'How did you do *that*?'

'Remember that Saturday when you thought I was going to the dentist? I went to the British Library instead. Looked up the newspaper archives.' A brief pause fell, and she hurried to break it. 'I'm sorry, Robert. I would have told you, it was just . . .'

'It's okay,' he said gently. 'I understand.'

'I just didn't want you to know I was thinking about him.' She stopped to sip her wine. 'It was easier to find than I'd expected. It was all over the papers, when his little sister got killed. They called it "The Vicarage Murder". Headlines for *weeks.*'

In the warm, airless night, Robert sat and watched her intently over the rim of his glass and didn't say a word.

'They arrested a man called Robert Harkness. He was a middle-aged man, bit of a loner. Strange-looking. The papers hated his guts,' said Marie. 'He went to prison for life. Killed himself there.'

Robert took a long deep breath. 'Poor sod.'

'No. You don't understand.' She paused, trying to collect her thoughts, untangle the issue. 'He killed her, Robert. It was an open-and-shut case.'

'How do you know?'

'You can't fake evidence like that. Even I know *that.* The skipping rope she was strangled with – his fingerprints were all over the handle. He was seen leaving the scene of the crime by three people.' She looked into the darkness of the garden – she might have been talking to the night. 'He confessed to it at the trial. Broke down and cried.'

Silence. Tense and seemingly endless silence.

'I don't know if he killed himself out of guilt,' she said at last. 'Maybe he was just scared of the other prisoners. But he was guilty, all right, Robert. No two ways about it.'

Robert's eyes were confused and uncomprehending. 'So what the hell did that note mean?'

'I don't know,' she said quietly. 'I suppose we never will.'

For long minutes, neither spoke. They sat and looked at each other in the pale misty floodlights, tableau-still. Far away, in the garden's black velvet shadows, something rustled.